He couldn't

He just couldn't!

He'd said his name was Rory. But...he hadn't admitted his last name.

Maddie's mind screamed for a logical explanation. Anything but the truth. Anything that would make this nightmare go away.

Neil March. The kind, gentle man named Rory who had been romancing her and little Nicky was Neil March, her sworn enemy.

She had very nearly given her heart to this man. Her foolish, foolish heart. Maddie couldn't bear to face the truth. The man who had given life and laughter back to her and her son was Neil March.

How could it be?

Award-winning author **Deb Kastner** writes stories of faith, family and community in a small-town Western setting. Deb's books contain sigh-worthy heroes and strong heroines facing obstacles that draw them closer to each other and the Lord. She lives in Colorado with her husband and is blessed with three daughters and two grandchildren. She enjoys spoiling her grandkids, movies, music (The Texas Tenors!), singing in the church choir and exploring Colorado on horseback.

Deb Kastner

A Holiday Prayer

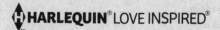

HARLEQUIN® *LOVE INSPIRED*®

Recycling programs
for this product may
not exist in your area.

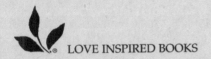

LOVE INSPIRED BOOKS

ISBN-13: 978-0-373-80385-9

A Holiday Prayer

As in water face reveals face,
so a man's heart reveals the man.
—*Proverbs* 27:19

To my three precious daughters,
Annie, Kimberly and Katie, who have
brought so much joy and meaning to my life.
Thank you for showing me every day
what it means to have faith as a child.

And to Keith and Dena Rice,
for the blessing and inspiration your music
and acting have been to me. Keith was the first,
and best, Phantom I've ever had the privilege
of seeing. Thanks to you both,
and to Mark Vogel, for granting me
the honor of using your song in this book.

Prologue

Have I not commanded you?
Be strong and courageous.
Do not be terrified; do not be discouraged,
for the Lord your God will be with you
wherever you go.

—Joshua 1:9

"Why won't they just leave me alone?"

Maddie Carlton glared at the offensive pile of gilt-edged invitations crammed through the mail slot of her town house, then shook her head at her bulldog, Max. "Don't they have anyone else to bother?" Max lifted his soulful eyes to her and shook his jowls.

"Yeah, that's what I thought," she mumbled. With a tired sigh, she bent down and retrieved her mail, tucking it under her arm as she shuffled into the kitchen. She hadn't bothered dressing for the day, and was still in a frayed gray terry-cloth bathrobe and matted slippers.

It was her mourning outfit.

She usually dressed and showered before waking her six-year-old son, Nicky, but today it was too much effort.

Christmas. Her first Christmas without Peter. And the anniversary of his death. All wrapped up in one morbid package.

The first months of grieving. Peter's birthday. Their wedding anniversary. Each date came and went, the sun rose and set, and Maddie was still walking and breathing, still cleaning and cooking—though sometimes it amazed her.

Life went on. But it was always a struggle.

It was Nicky who kept her rising every morning, moving through the day. For Nicky's sake she would do anything. Even get dressed when she felt like staying in bed, her head buried under mounds of covers.

With a cup of coffee to increase her fortitude, she slumped at the kitchen table, spreading her mail before her. Invitations, mostly.

Every charity this side of the Mississippi River had heard of her tragedy, and every one of them wanted to partake of her monetary settlement, the flower that they believed grew from the ashes.

Maddie snorted aloud, causing Max, who was trying to nap at her feet, to sniff and give her his best doggy put-down for disturbing his rest. If he could, Maddie thought, he'd be rolling his eyes. As it was, he groaned, rolled to his feet, turned his back on her and flopped to the floor again.

"Sorry, Max." She took a handful of envelopes and flipped through them. Who wanted her money today?

She was about to toss the whole unopened lot into "file thirteen" when a bright green envelope caught her eye. Usually the invitations and pleas came in fancy silver or burgundy, or at the very least in a crisp business envelope.

In addition to being a merry Christmas green, this envelope had a child's drawing of Santa and his reindeer.

Children's Hospital.

Even the name made her tremble. The other

envelopes dropped unnoticed to the floor as she ran a quivering finger across the seal.

For Children's Hospital, she would at least take a look.

Chapter One

Father, I cannot see tomorrow,
Father, I find it hard to pray,
Father, feeling these tears of sorrow,
Carry this weight... Show me the way.
Open up my eyes, Open up my ears,
Open up my heart.
Father, hear my prayer.

—Heartfelt

An ocean of masked partygoers washed toward the Brown Palace Hotel, their laughter echoing in the cold evening air. Maddie closed her eyes, trying to recall the feeling of gurgling laughter caught in her chest, bubbling up into her throat.

Her heart felt void of any emotion but a sense of apprehension at being in the public eye, of being recognized as the Wealthy Widow, as the newspapers had dubbed her.

Country-bred bumpkin was more like it, party clothes or no party clothes.

She stared in awe at the majestic exterior of the historic Brown Palace Hotel, a landmark sandwiched between office buildings in the heart of downtown Denver.

God help me. She sent up a silent prayer. *This isn't going to work without Your intervention.* She reached inside herself, searching for a snippet of peace that would make this night easier, but found nothing. Nothing. She was little more than an empty shell.

It had taken her years to adjust to being a suburban housewife on the outskirts of a big city, used as she was to her small hometown in eastern Colorado. No way would she ever fit in among an ostentatious crowd of silver-lined philanthropists. Even *with* a mask she was bound to give away her small-town roots.

Happily-ever-after storybook endings didn't exist. She was hard proof of that. Perhaps her sparkling Cinderella satin gown and glass slippers were more appropriate than she'd imagined. That irony crowned her, just as sure as the faux-diamond tiara she wore.

She wasn't looking for Prince Charming. She'd already had her one true love. Memories would have to be enough to bolster her through the remainder of life.

She ought to turn right around and go home where she belonged. She glanced back at the street, but the taxicab that had dropped her off in front of the hotel had long since vanished.

Maddie decided to walk back to 16th Street, where she could catch a bus back to her own neighborhood. She didn't really want to be alone in a crowd. Alone at home was easier to handle. She was still too used to having Peter by her side. Single was not her style.

And maybe it never would be.

She was looking at her see-through, plastic "glass" pumps, and didn't see the crowd approaching her until it was too late. A festive jumble of costumed people whirled her into their midst and, seeing she was also incognito, whisked her along with them into the hotel.

She fought to be released, but an older woman with a dozen glittering rings on one hand looped her arm through Maddie's, giving her little choice but to follow the others into the dark, panel-floored atrium. She sighed.

"'Nothing ventured, nothing gained,'" she quoted to herself.

"Exactly, dear," said the old woman with the rings, who stood at Maddie's side. Maddie had forgot that she wasn't alone, or she certainly wouldn't have spoken aloud. The gray-haired woman put a hand to Maddie's back and gave her a gentle nudge in the direction of the music. "Might as well take a peek, dear heart, since you've come this far."

The voice was filled with such authority that Maddie swiveled to catch her expression, but the woman was already tottering toward a group of friends, waving her arms enthusiastically at a big black bear.

She could see the second floor of the hotel through broad arches, and again felt a quiver of dismay at finding herself among a class of people who would frequent such a place. She felt like a church mouse in a grand cathedral.

Courage, Maddie, she mentally coaxed herself. *These people put their pants on the same way you do. Get a grip on it.*

She wandered tentatively into the ballroom, which had been transformed into a winter wonderland. Billowy cotton clouds hung from the ceiling, sequins glittering from their depths, and many-faceted paper snowflakes graced the walls. Pillarlike lamps wrapped with festive, pungent pine boughs surrounded the dance floor, giving the room a candlelit kind of glow. A twelve-piece orchestra played a lively Chopin waltz in one corner of the ballroom. Already, couples were whirling around the dance floor in time to the music.

The effect was magical, and Maddie experienced the temporary giddy feeling that she'd been transported to another time and place. Was this how Cinderella felt when she walked into the prince's palace? She took a deep breath and smoothed down the satiny folds of her opaque silver gown. *Cinderella.* Would it hurt to pretend? Just a little? And just this once?

Just for tonight, she promised herself. She was in a mask, after all, and had her hair and face made up. No one would recognize her. If the night went well, she might not even recognize herself.

Groups of chattering people mingled around the perimeter of the hall, while others sat at tables before plates mounded with food from the buffet in the next room. Everyone she saw was lavishly costumed—from a portly lion and his chair-wielding lion-tamer wife to Santa and Mrs. Claus.

What if one of the masked men in the room is Neil March? The unspoken question hit her with such sudden force that she nearly reeled. Her stomach tightened as she fought the nausea she felt every time she saw or heard his name.

It was Neil March's fault that she was here tonight. Alone.

Irrational though it might be, Maddie blamed Neil March for Peter's death. There was so much anger, so much pain. It had to be channeled somewhere and Maddie had, whether consciously or not, transferred her negative feelings to Neil March. He was, after all, the owner of the department store, and in her mind, that made him responsible.

The report by the fire department had cleared March's of any wrongdoing, but she clung stubbornly to her own suspicions. Authorities could be paid off to keep their findings a secret, and if there was one thing Neil March had plenty of, it was money. Hadn't he tried to buy her off, as well?

Her stomach clenched and she scanned the room in earnest.

What if he *was* here? Maddie gasped, fighting the waves of panic.

No. Neil March wouldn't be here. He was a playboy, not a philanthropist. What he'd paid her at Peter's untimely death had been nothing less than blood money. Not offered out of generosity. And definitely not offered out of compassion. Of that she was certain.

Though she knew him to be a practiced businessman, she pictured Neil as a young, arrogant preppy, complete with khaki pants and a designer polo shirt with the collar flipped up on his neck. He'd have a tennis racket slung over one arm and a gorgeous blonde on the other.

She didn't recall seeing any preppy tennis players here tonight mingling among the guests.

She snorted at her own joke. It was the closest she'd come to laughing since Peter had died. The sober thought dropped the smile from her lips.

Neil March was certainly nothing to laugh about.

"Excuse me." She flagged down a passing waiter. "Do you have water?" She realized she sounded like a dehydrated camel after days in the desert, but the waiter remained straight-faced. "Of course, madam."

Moments later she was gulping down a glass of water, coughing and sputtering when it went down wrong. She pounded a fist against her chest to dislodge what felt like a boulder. "Maddie, you *have* to relax!" she muttered under her breath.

"Hey! Check it out. Now *that's* a costume and a half!" a young blonde in a tennis outfit said, grabbing Maddie by the elbow.

There went her theory that there were no tennis players here tonight. The young woman was the gorgeous blonde half of her Neil March scenario, with white culottes that put the *short* in shorts. Bleach-blond hair and a knockout tan in the dead of winter?

Intrigued, Maddie looked to where the blonde was pointing her tennis racket. Something had clearly captured her attention.

Standing in the doorway, his feet braced and hands on his hips, was the Phantom of the Opera, handsome despite the fact that the upper half of his face was masked in stark white.

She was immediately struck by his impressive bearing and thick, broad shoulders. His black cutaway tuxedo was covered with a many-caped greatcoat, fastened at the neck amid snowy-white ruffles. His presence was intense and powerful, and Maddie could see that she wasn't the only woman inexplicably drawn to his mask and the thick black hair curling down around his collar.

He appeared to be looking for someone, his strong, thin lips turned down at the corners in just the shadow of a frown.

His gaze passed where she stood, then moved back again, as if he were taking a second look. No doubt he was, since Ms. Short-shorts was still holding on to Maddie's elbow. She was exactly the sort of woman to make a man do a double take.

Maddie wasn't surprised when he strode toward them. The young woman dropped her tennis racket to her side and stood with one hand on her hip, greeting the Phantom with a brilliant smile.

Oddly enough, Maddie had the peculiar sensation that he was watching *her,* coming for *her,* as if he'd picked an old friend's face from a crowd. And it sent shivers down her spine. But of course that was nonsense. He was coming for the blonde.

With unconscious grace, he unhooked the

cape and swung it around, folding it across a chair. Maddie's heart leaped to her throat, and she nearly dropped the water glass that she held in her hand. This man was *definitely* not an old friend.

She would have remembered such a compelling gaze, the way his dark eyes burned through the stark whiteness of the mask...and especially that confident swagger that caught the attention of every woman he passed.

Her head spun as the man grew nearer. She was vaguely aware of the sound of her own breath heavy in her ears, the pounding of her heart in her head.

Now he was in front of her, looking straight at her. As if he knew her. But there was no way he could recognize her through her mask. And even if he could see her face, it was improbable that he'd know her. How could he? She wasn't part of this crowd.

Perhaps that was the problem. Did she stick out like a weed among orchids? Maybe she looked like the grungy suburban housewife that she was, as out of place as a child at a grown-up party.

He grinned then, the smile starting at his lips and emanating from his obsidian-black eyes behind the mask. His smile encompassed both Maddie and the primping blonde at her side.

So that was it. He was being polite, figuring Maddie was Ms. Short-shorts's friend. And he was probably wondering how to get rid of her.

Well, she'd make it easy for him. She didn't know why Goldilocks had latched on to her in the first place, and she had no qualms about bowing out when she wasn't wanted. She dislodged her elbow from the blonde's grasp just as the Phantom held out his hand and gestured toward the dance floor.

Let's move it, sweetie. He's obviously asking you to dance, and he isn't going to wait forever, Maddie thought uncharitably, wondering why the woman's grip on her elbow had tightened. What was this woman's problem? *Not* a tough decision, especially for one as used to society charity balls as this girl seemed to be.

She glanced to her side. The young woman stared at Maddie with a mixture of disbelief and pique, then glanced at the Phantom. She swung her astonished gaze to Maddie and, with an unladylike snort, flounced away in a huff.

Either the woman was crazy, or a complete

idiot. And the Phantom had just been jilted. She turned to the man and offered a regretful shrug and a tentative smile.

The dark-haired man combed his fingers through the curls at the back of his neck. "Well?"

Maddie cocked her head. "Well?" she repeated.

"Dance with me."

His voice was as low and rich as she'd imagined it would be. And she had definitely imagined the words.

Dance?

His eyes lit with amusement at her hesitation.

"Weren't you asking Goldilocks to dance?" she blurted.

"Who?" The Phantom looked genuinely perplexed.

"You know." Maddie tipped her head in the direction the blonde had disappeared. "The tennis player."

The Phantom chuckled. "Not a chance. She's a little young. And definitely not my type. I was asking *you* to dance."

He was asking her to dance. And the orchestra was breaking into a slow ballad even as they spoke.

She nodded and took the hand he extended.

She felt a twinge of guilt when he swept her into his arms. It felt awkward. She hadn't danced in ages. And for so many years it had only been Peter.

Peter's arms. Peter's whisper.

She felt the electric heat of the Phantom's hand on her hip and her mind clicked into gear. A wave of panic surged over her.

Oh, Lord, what have I gotten into now?

She'd come here to support Children's Hospital, not to dance. It was too much, too fast. To be dancing in another man's arms, feeling another man's heartbeat against her palm. Guilt turned the screw. Was she betraying Peter's memory?

But Peter was gone. The Phantom was here, and his light embrace was not unpleasant. Besides, it was only one dance.

While Peter couldn't dance to save his life, the Phantom was clearly a dancer, swaying easily in time to the music. Peter had been lean and lank, but her fingers now burned with the feel of the Phantom's thick, rippling biceps. And he was shorter than Peter had been, though still a good head taller than Maddie. She would, she thought with an uncomfortable flutter of her stomach, fit right into the crook of the man's shoulder.

As if he read her thoughts, he smiled at her.

At last, an imperfection. She was beginning to think that he was perfect in form and face—or at least what she could see of it. But his smile was crooked and little-boy adorable.

He chuckled low in his chest and his dark eyes sparkled with mirth. He lowered his head until his warm breath tickled the sensitive skin of her neck, sending shivers of delight down her spine. "You're staring at me."

Maddie felt as if he'd jolted her with a white-hot bolt of electricity. With a whimper of dismay, she attempted to shrug out of his arms.

His hand on her hip tightened in response. "Don't run," he implored in a throaty whisper. "Please. I was only kidding."

She grimaced and tittered nervously. "I apologize. It's just that I…"

He lifted his hand from her hip and gently placed his forefinger over her lips. "No. You don't have to explain. Just dance with me."

She nodded, losing track of her thoughts in liquid black eyes reminiscent of some Native

American ancestor and confirmed by his angular features and aquiline nose.

He shifted slightly, pulling her into his chest so that his hand now rested at the small of her back. It was a modest gesture, but enough for her to feel the rock-hard ripples of his shoulder under her cheek.

She inhaled deeply, then fought the sense of guilt assaulting her even as the faint spice of the Phantom's aftershave made her nostrils tingle.

Oh, God, she prayed as grief washed over her. How she missed Peter.

Deep inside her heart, the part of her that had agonized through every lonely night, mourning Peter's death, facing the achingly empty king-size bed alone, struggling through empty days, needed to move closer into the embrace of her Phantom gentleman.

She was relieved that he wasn't trying to make idle conversation. She didn't want to talk. She just wanted to be held. If only for a moment. To feel the brush of warm breath tickle her ear. To revel in strong arms encircling her waist.

But how could she?

She pulled back, opening the space between

them. She should turn around and walk away. This instant, while she still had the strength to do so.

The Phantom's warm hand lightly resting on her back sent shivers up her spine that had nothing to do with cold. Her spirit soared.

With a deep inner sigh, she allowed him to draw her closer. Being in his arms felt good and right. She would face her regrets tomorrow.

For tonight, she was going to dance.

Chapter Two

The Phantom leaned back to study the petite woman in his arms. Her face, framed by cinnamon-brown hair, was rosy with color. In her silvery ball gown and glass slippers she made a perfect Cinderella.

Though he still wasn't certain why, she'd caught his eye the moment he had entered the ballroom. Perhaps it was because she looked small, and shy, and completely ill at ease.

He suspected that there was a latent fireman in him someplace, because she looked just like a little lost kitten stranded in a treetop. He felt like grabbing a ladder and rescuing her. Putting a smile on her heart-shaped face, a sparkle in her shadowed brown eyes.

He shifted forward so he could feel the satin softness of her cheek against his. Immediately, he felt her muscles bunch as if she were preparing to spring from his grasp.

She seemed as jumpy as a jackrabbit being chased by a fox. But if she wanted to run away, he couldn't bring himself to let her go. There was something familiar about her—something he couldn't name, but which compelled him to keep her close.

He hadn't even planned to come to the benefit in the first place. He rarely went out anymore.

And he *never* danced. What had drawn him onto the dance floor was as much a mystery to him as was the woman in his arms.

It didn't matter, anyway. He was here now. And he didn't plan to leave. Or to let her go.

His face lingered near her bare shoulder, inhaling her light, musky fragrance. She wasn't smothered in expensive perfume like most women of his acquaintance. No. She smelled like…

Moonlight.

If there were any way to blot out the nightmare of thoughts haunting him, it would be this beautiful woman.

He leaned back and smiled down at her, feeling her body stiffen when his gaze met hers.

Why was she so afraid?

His throat tightened at the look of utter helplessness in her huge brown eyes, and he became suddenly determined to change the course of her evening.

Before the night was through, he vowed to himself, he would hear the sweet sound of her laughter.

Maddie expected him to release her after the song ended, but he continued to sway back and forth as if the orchestra continued to play. She glanced around the room, terrified that she was making a spectacle of herself, but no one seemed to notice the still-dancing couple.

Moments later she heard the shrill wail of a saxophone and sagged with relief as the Phantom adjusted their steps to the beat of the new song. He was obviously determined to enjoy the evening. With her.

Well, so was she. With him.

"What's your name?" he whispered into her ear.

Maddie stepped back and curtsied playfully. "I thought you would have guessed by now," she teased. "Cinderella, of course!"

The Phantom let out a full-bodied laugh that

caused those dancing around them to peer at them curiously.

"We're going to play games, are we?" He took a step back and gave an elegant bow. "I guess that would make me your Phantom."

Maddie was more than content to leave the introductions at that. They would all unmask at midnight, after all. If she stayed that long....

She had a sneaking suspicion she just might.

For the moment she was content just to remain in his arms and lose herself in the music. It was pure magic, and she didn't intend to waste a single moment.

The song came to a close and the orchestra's lead violist surprised everyone by breaking out in a fiddling tune. In moments a country line dance was formed.

Her Phantom chuckled and drew her to the edge of the floor. "Sorry, love. I don't do country."

Maddie shrugged. It wasn't hard to smile. Country wasn't her style, either. "I'm ready for a break."

The Phantom indicated a chair and held it for her, while she gathered her skirts and sat. "Are you thirsty? Why don't I get you some..." His sentence trailed off.

She looked up, surprised. His eyes were cloudy and unreadable. He seemed to be sidetracked by something at the far corner of the ballroom.

She followed his gaze but saw nothing out of the ordinary. Unless it was one of a number of beautiful young women over there.

She replied, "No, that's okay. I'm not thirsty."

But the Phantom was not listening. He was already walking away from her, his mind obviously elsewhere. As if with great effort, he tossed one quick glance back at her. "Excuse me. I'll just…"

And then he was gone.

Maddie sighed and crossed her arms over her chest, though she could feel a hesitant smile still hovering on her lips.

Her fantasy was over. And she really should be angry with the man for abandoning her so abruptly. But the lovely warmth, telling her that she still had a heart, lingered. She felt alive, really alive, for the first time in years.

There would be no regrets. It didn't matter that she'd been deserted for fresher prey. She was more than content just to sit here and watch wildly costumed dancers wiggling to some latest craze in line dancing.

One young man, dressed most appropriately as a rooster, was crowing loudly and shaking his tail feathers in wild abandon. The music did sound rather like a clucking chicken.

She felt a small rumble building deep in her chest, growing promptly into full-fledged laughter. She clapped a hand over her mouth to keep from appearing rude.

But not to stem the flow of laughter. It felt so good—better even than whirling around on the dance floor. She felt like leaping up and shaking her own tail feathers.

Laughter scoured her insides clean. Maybe she'd get really brave and find a partner for one last dance.

"That chicken is really something." The rich, soft, unmistakable baritone came from behind her, next to her ear. Her Phantom was back.

Her heart leaped into her throat, her head buzzing with excitement and the purely female thrill of attracting a handsome man. Not once, but twice. "Yes, he is, isn't he?"

The Phantom chuckled. "I meant the music. It's called 'The Chicken.' I guess 'cause it sounds like a chicken clucking."

Maddie grinned. "I noticed."

"What do you say we get out of here for a while?" he whispered.

It had been a few years, but his words sounded distinctly like a come-on. She cocked her eyebrow. "Out?"

He grinned and held up his hands as if to ward off her unspoken accusation. "Just out for a breath of air and some peace and quiet. That's all. I promise. Promise."

"Oh, but they're going to unmask at midnight!" she protested, though it sounded weak, even to her. She was being worn down, and his wink told her that he knew it. But she really did want to dance again before she left. Desperately.

"Never fear. We'll be back before then. Come on, let's get some air."

Maddie cast one last disappointed glance at the dance floor, then shrugged. It wouldn't hurt to leave for a few minutes. And he'd promised to be back before they unmasked. She hoped they'd have one more dance together before the night ended.

He led her to the door and assisted her with her coat. "I've got a surprise for you."

"Surprise?" she repeated lamely, and then wondered at the wisdom of following an unknown man onto the streets of downtown Denver. A woman couldn't be too careful. And she was no innocent child.

She searched his eyes for some sign of his intentions, but found only a gleam of humor lurking in their black depths. He wasn't giving anything away.

At least not yet. But he wasn't the least bit threatening.

He raised a questioning eyebrow over the top of the mask.

The decision was hers. She glanced back into the ballroom and the safety it represented.

The Phantom stood patiently, arms crossed over his thick chest and a half smile lingering on his lips. She had the niggling impression that he sensed the dilemma she was working through and was certain of the outcome.

She stood undecided for a moment more, knowing what she would do and waiting for the rational part of her brain to call her an impulsive fool. She instinctively trusted her Phantom. He was strong, but gentle. If she were going to gamble with her safety, she would bet on this man.

She nodded slowly. "All right. Let's go."

A gust of crisp Christmas air hit them as

they stepped out of the hotel, causing Maddie's lungs to burn. It was a pleasant sensation, she decided. She carefully watched her steps on the icy pavement. Glass slippers weren't exactly winter-weather gear, and she found herself wishing she'd worn her thick leather snow boots.

She slipped and giggled. The Phantom quickly clasped her arm, but not fast enough to keep her from sliding unceremoniously to the ground in a heap. The picture of herself in a satin dress and snow boots sent her into another fit of giggles.

It felt good. Very good.

"Your surprise...." the Phantom reminded her.

He reached a hand to help her to her feet, then pointed at the curb. Her heart pounded as she got her first hint of the Phantom's scheme, which was at that moment stomping its impatience into the pavement. She clapped a hand over her mouth and exclaimed in delight over the slick white horse-drawn carriage, complete with a liveried driver.

"Oh, it's lovely!" she exclaimed as he settled her on the seat and wrapped a wool blanket around her legs. "But aren't we going to freeze?"

The Phantom chuckled and draped an arm around her shoulders. "No chance of that. We'll just take a short ride down the 16th Street Mall. Have you seen the Christmas lights yet? They're gorgeous this time of night."

Maddie shook her head. This was truly a night she would remember for a long time to come. If she believed in fairy tales, she'd think she stepped right into one. Even the crisp air couldn't dull the heat warming her cheeks.

Motioning for the driver to stop, her Phantom gestured at the forty-three-foot Christmas tree in Larimer Square, the largest to be found in Denver.

"Didn't I tell you it was beautiful?" he whispered, his breath fanning her cheek.

She turned her face toward him, expecting him to be watching the Christmas display, hoping to be able to study his masked face. His eyes met hers, and she suddenly realized that he'd been watching her, seeing the wonders of Christmas in downtown Denver through her, sharing in her delight.

Her breath mingled with his, their lips only inches apart. His dark, intense gaze probed hers. It would take only the merest action on her part…just a shimmer of movement and their lips would meet.

Dragging in a breath, she turned away. How could she even consider…? But she had. She did. Guilt ripped through her like a rudder blade on the snow.

She had no right. And even less sense.

"Drive on," her Phantom commanded, leaning back in the seat. She was afraid to look at him, afraid of what she would see in his eyes.

If only he would take that blasted mask off and she could see him as a real human being instead of the larger-than-life Phantom of the Opera. It was just that fairy-tale feeling again, getting the best of her. He was only a man underneath that mask. A plain, ordinary man. Maybe even disguising some hidden flaw.

The corner of her lips quivered into a smile.

"A penny for your thoughts," he whispered. On the inside of her wrist, he planted a tiny kiss that radiated heat up the entire length of her arm.

She tried to ignore the sensation. "As if I'd sell them so cheap."

The Phantom lifted an eyebrow. He was intrigued by this bright-eyed Cinderella, more so than he wanted to put a value to. "A million dollars, then."

She stiffened.

"What? What did I say?" He'd been teasing, but by the look on her face, he could tell he'd said the wrong thing. She went as hot and then cold as a kitchen tap.

"Nothing."

Nothing. No more than she had told him all evening. And why should it matter? He wasn't in the market for a relationship. He should be glad she wasn't pressing him.

But he wasn't glad.

Who *was* this woman? He'd been stretching his mind for the answer, but the mask continued to throw him. He'd seen her somewhere— he knew he had.

But how to coax her from her shell? Flattery didn't work. With a teasing lilt to his voice, he appealed. "Tell me your name."

Maddie's brown eyes sparkled mischievously. "Not just yet. You'll find out soon enough, in any case." She gently removed her arm from his grasp and laced her fingers together on her lap. "Tell me about you."

"Okay," he agreed easily, leaning back into the cushion and laying his arm over the back of the seat. Perhaps if he opened up, she would feel more comfortable revealing something about herself. He barely dared to hope.

"I work for a large company in the area. I play racquetball and golf. I like pizza and Pepsi. Anything else you want to know?"

"My, my," Maddie bantered. "Vague, aren't we? A large company in the area? That hardly narrows it down. What kind of business?"

"Enough about me," he countered, combing his fingers through the curls on his neck. "Tell me about you."

Maddie didn't want to talk about herself. Not tonight. She lifted her chin. If he could be stubborn, so could she.

The Phantom chuckled again. "We all have secrets, don't we?" he said before tapping the driver on the shoulder. "A rose for the lady, please."

The driver nodded and pulled to the side of the road, gesturing to one of the many corner flower vendors peddling their wares to the late-night Christmas shoppers. "I need a rose," he rasped.

The Phantom presented the single, long-stemmed red rose to Maddie with an endearingly crooked grin. "A beautiful flower for a beautiful lady."

Maddie's breath caught in her throat. "I… I…"

The Phantom frowned and he rolled his eyes.

"What?" Maddie asked in surprise.

"I think I've just blurted out the most inane line in history. And it's all your fault. One look at you and my mind gets all mixed up."

He was teasing her, she knew, but nonetheless she could feel the heat staining her cheeks crimson. She took refuge in inhaling the rose's intoxicating scent. The petals still had moisture on them, and they glistened in the dull light of the streetlamps.

"Won't you tell me your name?" he pleaded quietly, his rich baritone rolling over each syllable. "We're going to unmask soon, anyway. What difference will a few minutes make?"

She stared at her hands clasped in her lap. Maybe he was right. What was the difference? She glanced over at him, but he was staring off into the distance. "Maddie Carlton," she whispered, her breath misting the air.

His gaze snapped to hers, boring into her with such intensity that Maddie felt suffocated.

"You've heard of me," she said quietly, removing the now unnecessary mask from her face. "I lost my husband in the March's Department Store fiasco last Christmas. My only claim to fame is that Neil March settled me with a ridiculous amount of money."

The Phantom's jaw tightened and he looked away. She could see the tension lining his face, causing the muscles in his neck to strain against his cravat.

Maddie unconsciously leaned away from him, wondering what she'd said that had set him off.

He obviously didn't like what he heard. He probably expected her to be some debutante from old money, not a widow with a tragic past and a son to boot.

Well, the truth had to come out sooner or later. There was nothing she could do about it if he was disappointed. None of this was real, anyway.

His eyes became dull and shaded, the fire in his eyes extinguished as effectively as if it had been doused with water.

The fairy tale was over, blown sky-high by her own big mouth. She should have kept her identity a secret, she silently reprimanded her-

self. She should have extended the fantasy—
for what it was worth—as long as possible.

She stared out onto the darkened street and
sighed deeply, remembering. She hadn't even
threatened March with a lawsuit or anything.
She hadn't wanted a penny of his money. It had
just showed up in the mail one day—a certi-
fied check for half a million dollars. The first
of six checks! Even now she found it hard to
comprehend.

She turned back to face him, wondering at
his silence.

His dark eyes were full of a mixture of regret and— What was it? Pain? Anger?

She never had the opportunity to find out.

Tapping the driver on the shoulder, he demanded the carriage be stopped. "I've got to
go." The words were softly spoken but cut into
Maddie's heart as if he'd screamed.

He cleared his throat, then shook his head as
if he had decided against explaining further.
Tentatively, he reached forward, brushing the
inside of his thumb along her cheek in a featherlight caress.

"I..." he said, his voice husky. He leaned
forward, his eyes never leaving hers. For Mad-

die, time moved in slow motion as she waited breathlessly for his lips to meet hers.

When the moment came, she closed her eyes, savoring every touch, every sensation, storing up for the long, empty nights ahead. His lips were cool and firm, but his breath was warm.

With a sigh, he leaned forward, deepening the kiss, just for a moment.

Maddie wanted to cling to him, but she clenched her hands in her lap, willing them not to betray her, shaking so hard that she was sure he could feel it.

"Oh, Maddie," he whispered against her lips, the words deep and razor-sharp.

She opened her eyes when he abruptly pushed away from her, the sweet taste of his kiss still lingering on her lips.

Without another word, he jumped out of the carriage and strode away, disappearing into the darkness.

Chapter Three

Maddie sighed and brushed a stray tendril of hair from her forehead. She felt hot and sweaty and her muscles ached from carrying boxes up from the basement. Yet she hadn't ventured to open a single one of the cartons that now filled her living room.

It was the handwriting scribbled in wide, black marker ink that stopped her.

Peter's handwriting.

Christmas. The boxes set aside for the happiest time of year, laden with bright and glittering decorations that she knew would delight her young son.

But the sight of the festive decorations had no effect on her, except maybe to tighten the vise around her heart.

She wasn't happy. And she didn't know if

she could fake it, even for Nicky. Could she really put together a six-foot artificial tree by herself? Never mind lift Nicky to place the angel on top—a tradition formerly and laughingly performed by Peter.

She muttered a prayer for help, but it smacked against the ceiling of her apartment and came showering down again in thousands of tiny pieces. Or at least that's how it felt to her.

She was living in a tiny wooden crate with no air and no light. She'd been abandoned. First by her father. Then by Peter. And now, it seemed, even God had left her to flounder on her own.

Madelaine Anne! She could hear her mother's voice as if it were yesterday. *If you can't find God, it's because you've backed off. He hasn't gone anywhere.*

She toyed with the idea of making a phone call. Mom always knew what to say. But Maddie's faith wasn't as strong as her mother's. In fact, she wasn't sure if she had faith at all. Would someone with real faith question what God had done?

Maddie did. Every single day. Peter's death didn't make any more sense to her now than it had a year ago. Even the newspapers had called it a senseless tragedy.

God is in control.

If that was true, why hadn't she even been able to find a crack in the woodwork of this crate of hers?

Except, perhaps, last night. Last night, for one brief, shining moment, she had remembered what it was like to laugh. The deep melodic voice of her Phantom rang through her memory, and she smiled. He had given her a precious gift. He had helped her laugh again. She would always be grateful to him for that.

Her smile faded. Last night it had been easy to think about celebrating Christmas again. Last night she'd even believed she might enjoy the festive spirit, revel in the preparations.

But not now. Not with all these boxes as glaring reminders of the love she and Peter had shared, love that had brought her dear Nicky into the world.

She would not cry.

And she would *not* let Nicky down. He deserved a memorable Christmas. And if God *was* here, she was going to give Nicky the best Christmas of his life.

She gritted her teeth against the waves

of nausea in her stomach and the ferocious pounding in her head. The huge box containing the Christmas tree was waiting for her attention. With a deep breath for courage, she plunged her arms in, triumphantly emerging with an armful of tree limbs in various shapes and sizes.

After five minutes of work, she'd managed to find the tree base, and had buried herself knee-deep in branches.

She'd never paid the least attention to Peter when he put the tree together, but if he could do it, so could she. Didn't the dumb tree come with instructions?

She burst into frustrated tears. What a stupid thing to cry over, she reprimanded herself. But she didn't try to brush the tears away. If it wasn't this, it would be something else. She hadn't realized how much she depended on Peter.

And now she was alone.

"Why did you leave me, Peter? Why? I never was good enough for you, was I?" The words echoed in the empty room, an echo answered in her empty heart.

She scrubbed a determined hand down her face, resolving to divide and conquer. No stupid artificial tree would get the best of her, even if it took her all day to assemble.

Her lips pinched with determination, she leaned into the box until she felt as though she were being swallowed. She groped around the bottom, her fingers nimbly searching for anything resembling paper, but found nothing but a stray line of garland.

What might Peter have done with the instructions?

Tossed them.

The thought caught her by surprise and she barked out a laugh. Of course. That's *exactly* what her handyman husband would have done. In his opinion, written instructions were the bane of a "real" man's existence, to be scoffed at and referred to only as a last resort.

Which left her with a gigantic tree-size problem. Hands on her hips, she surveyed the limb-strewn room.

Christmas music. She'd throw on a CD of favorite Christmas tunes for a little holiday spirit. Maybe all she needed was to set the mood. Though she thought it highly improbable that the tree would put itself together even *with* the proper ambience.

"Oh, Mama!" Nicky exclaimed, scuffling

sleepily from his bedroom. He was still clad in his superhero pajamas, his white-blond hair rumpled from sleep. "A Christmas tree!"

Her heart warmed at the sight of her son's glowing eyes. It was worth any amount of pain to give her son some joy in his life. And perhaps—if God were merciful—she could partake in a moment or two of Christmas joy herself.

She wanted to wrap her arms around him in a bear hug, but knew he would take that as a personal assault on his big-boy dignity. Instead, she ruffled his hair. "Well, it's supposed to be."

She laughed as Nicky threw himself into a pile of limbs as if it were a mountain of crisp autumn leaves.

"As you can see, Mom's having a little bit of trouble putting this thing together."

Nicky's expression became serious, his brows knit together. "I'll help."

The look was so much his father's that Maddie's throat tightened.

Nicky began gathering limbs in his stout little arms. "Look, Mom. They have colors on the ends."

Hmm. So they did. How had she missed

something so patently obvious? She couldn't say, but she felt the heat rising in her cheeks. Leave it to her six-year-old son to solve the problem before she did.

She picked up one of the smaller branches, marked with yellow paint on the end that stuck into the base. "These yellow ones must go on top."

Humming along with "Jingle Bells," she began poking the metal end into the top of the base. They'd have a Christmas tree yet. And maybe even before the new year hit!

"No, Mama. The big branches first. That's how Daddy always used to do it."

Tears sprang again to her eyes, and she quickly brushed them away before her son could see. How could he possibly remember Peter putting up the Christmas tree? It had been two years—two achingly painful years— since there'd been no tree last year. Last year they'd celebrated Christmas in Children's Hospital.

How could Nicky possibly remember that far back? He would have been four, watching Peter with wide-eyed wonder and the universal childhood belief that Daddy could do anything.

But somehow, he remembered.

She cleared her throat against the pain choking the breath from her lungs. The picture of flames engulfing the Santa's workshop display overwhelmed her, as if she were trapped in a theater, forced to watch the same movie over and over. She could smell the acrid smoke... hear her son screaming.

Daddy. Daddy. Daddy!

"Mom?" Nicky pulled on the sleeve of her sweatshirt. "Mom? Are you okay?"

She shook her head to clear the memories. "We're going to the zoo tonight," she said a little too brightly, forcing her mind to shift gears.

"Will we get to see the elephants?" Nicky asked, excitement brimming from his eyes and voice.

Maddie nodded. "Yes, honey. We'll get to see some very special elephants. They're opening the new Pachyderm Pavilion tonight, and we get to be the first ones to see it."

"What's a pack-eee-drum?"

She laughed and hugged her bouncing, squirming child to her chest. "It means elephants, I think. And maybe rhinos, too. Can you guess why the Pachyderm Pavilion is so special?"

Nicky nodded solemnly. "My teacher told

us at school. It has Daddy's name on it, right, Mom?"

"Right, sweetheart. And that's why we get to be the first ones to go inside!"

"Do you think I can feed one of the elephants?"

"I don't know about that. But it wouldn't hurt to ask. You're Peter Carlton's son, after all."

"Yesss!" Nicky bunched his fist and brought his elbow into his hip.

"I think I can safely promise you can feed the ducks. Now, why don't we try and get this Christmas tree up before Christmas has come and gone. Can you help me sort the branches into piles?"

Neil March pulled his wool coat more tightly around his chest and stared dully at the pond where ducks quacked and vied for his attention. The bridge he stood on elevated his contact with the biting wind, and he shivered.

He shouldn't be here. It was too risky. What if she saw him? Then she would know....

But he could no more keep himself from coming tonight than he could stop his heart from beating. He had to see her. At least one more time.

He'd stay well hidden. She'd be busy with the press. There was no way she'd spot him in the crowd. And it wasn't as if she would recognize his face.

She would never have to know the truth.

The air was bitterly cold. He glanced up at the sky, wondering idly if it was going to snow.

He didn't know why anyone would want to come to see the Denver Zoo's Wildlights in this nasty weather—but the park was crowded. Probably the grand opening of the elephant exhibit lured them in. It had been well publicized.

As for him…he was here for her. There was no sense denying it. He was here because he couldn't stand the thought of going through life without looking once more into those sparkling brown eyes.

He wanted so much more, but that was impossible for him. For them. They had barriers between them that made the Great Wall of China pale in comparison. Walls of which she knew nothing, and of which he knew too much.

His life was spiraling from painful to unbearable since meeting Maddie face-to-face, and he could do nothing to stop it. How could he? He deserved to suffer.

He was, after all, responsible for the accident, for the fire, for his store going up in flames. And ultimately, for Peter Carlton's death. He'd have to live with that knowledge for the rest of his life.

With all the strength of his will, he pushed his mind from the future. And from the past. Brooding wouldn't help matters.

At least he had tonight. Another chance to look at her. To see her shining eyes and glowing face. To listen to the sultry hum of her voice.

Even if she didn't know he was there.

He wondered why she had given so much money to the zoo. Not that he begrudged her the money. He was glad she was spending it, remembering all too well her refusal to sully her hands with his pathetic attempt at atonement. As if anything could make her life better.

It was his fault that she was alone, and the guilt pierced his heart like a lance.

Why had she chosen elephants? They had been his childhood favorite, both at the zoo and the circus. Perhaps her son had chosen where the money went.

Or had they been Peter Carlton's favorite, too?

A mallard swam up to the bridge and quacked loudly, flapping his wings for attention.

Neil glanced at his watch. He had a few minutes left before he needed to join the crowd heading toward the pavilion for the grand opening.

Fishing in his pocket for change, Neil smiled. "You're in luck, Duck. I happen to have a quarter. And I happen to be in a good mood."

It wasn't exactly the truth. But it would have to do. He put the coin in the machine dispensing duck pellets and cranked the handle.

He didn't have much to offer. But at least he could feed the ducks.

Chapter Four

❧

"Mom, look! The polar bear is going for a swim!" Wildlights at the Zoo was a yearly tradition for the Carltons. Adults and children alike enjoyed seeing the animals at night, and the zoo blazing with Christmas color.

Maddie shivered. That polar bear was clean out of his mind, lumbering into the icy water as if he were taking a cool dip in summertime. Give or take a few hours and he might be able to ice-skate on his pool.

If it wasn't so cold, she might really be enjoying herself. But the nip of the wind stole away any pleasure she might have had. Nicky, bouncing with energy, didn't seem to notice, and dashed away to the next display. It was all she could do to keep up with the boy.

She followed him halfheartedly, her mind wandering back to the previous evening.

Last night. What had she been doing at this time last night?

She glanced at her watch.

Dancing. She'd been dancing with her Phantom.

A deep sigh escaped her lips. All she had left of the night was the rose, carefully pressed and drying between the pages of her journal. Were it not for that, Maddie might have thought that it had all been some incredible romantic dream. Like Cinderella's glass slipper, the rose was a memento to remember the occasion by.

She wished she'd given him something, as well. It would be nice to think that there was a man out there somewhere who remembered her as glamorous Cinderella, and not as a pain-stricken widow.

It was just as well that he'd forever remain a Phantom, she reflected as she led her son to the next zoo display. Any more time in the company of the masked man would no doubt have revealed some all-too-real faults that would have brought her crashing back to reality.

He was much better left a dream.

With gigantic effort, she thrust her thoughts

back into the present. "Do you want to feed the ducks?" Maddie asked, ruffling her son's white-blond locks. "We've still got a few minutes before we need to head for the elephants."

Loaded with a pocketful of quarters, Nicky shouted and raced for the bridge, and to the machine offering duck pellets. He was tossing them by the fistful at the ducks when Maddie strolled up, breathing heavily of the crisp winter air.

Silently watching Nicky calling to the ducks, a man leaned out over the bridge. His dark hair and the set of his broad shoulders seemed achingly familiar, making butterflies dance in Maddie's stomach.

She stopped short. It couldn't be him. The thought was utterly ridiculous. What would a wealthy businessman be doing at the zoo, and alone at that? She chastised her fickle mind for betraying her.

She was going crazy, that's what it was. She'd spent one pleasant evening with a man, and now that she had returned to reality, and was alone once again, she was conjuring him up from the depths of her mind and projecting him onto a stranger.

Desperation at its ugliest. She needed to get

a grip on her emotions. And concentrate on her son.

She gave the man one last glance, hoping that by doing so she could prove to her flighty emotions that she was making something out of nothing. It wasn't him. It couldn't be him. And her eyes would prove it.

As the ducks clamored around Nicky, she heard the rich sound of the man's chuckle. And then he combed his fingers through the curls at his neck.

Her heart quavered and dropped into her toes. Her mind screamed, both in elation and disbelief. It was the one gesture that would forever be etched in her mind—the heart-stopping idiosyncrasy of her Phantom.

Unbidden, anger welled in her chest. He'd abandoned her, and he had never let her see his face. How dare he disappear without a word?

Well, she had some words for him! Persuading her to unmask, and then refusing to do the same. Running off on her without even saying goodbye. Who was it that said women were fickle? It must have been a *man*.

She stomped forward and yanked on the wool of his coat, pulling him around to face her.

When her gaze met his intense, flaming

eyes, she gasped. The tiny, niggling voice still whispering that it might not be the same man died a quick and silent death as recognition lit his dark eyes and a crooked smile replaced his frown.

It was her Phantom.

She hadn't even considered the fact that he wouldn't be wearing a mask, or given a thought to what he might look like without it. In her spontaneous rush of anger, she'd approached him without thinking, both dreading and anticipating the confrontation.

She stepped back in shock at what she saw. His strong cheekbones, which had been hidden by the mask, gave even more depth to the planes of his face. He was, as she had known he would be, strikingly handsome.

But that wasn't what made her gasp. His mask had indeed been hiding the truth.

The right side of his face, around the temple, forehead and eye, was covered with very real bandages.

Surprise registered only momentarily on his face before he grinned and shrugged. "I see you caught me. Your Phantom is more like the real Phantom of the Opera than you anticipated, huh?"

Maddie tried to speak, but her mouth was dry. "I…uh…"

"I'm sorry. I can see I startled you. I—"

"Mom! I fed *all* of the ducks!" Nicky bounded between them, bouncing on his toes.

"He did, too!" her Phantom confirmed, smiling in a way that made Maddie's heart turn over. Something about those lips. Perhaps it was the bandages that shadowed the rest of his face, just as the Phantom's mask had. Or maybe she was remembering the sweet tenderness of his kiss.

She shook her head, trying to dispel the thought. Nicky latched on to her arm and peered timidly at the bandage-faced man. "It's okay, Nicky. This man is my—" she hesitated over the word "—friend."

"I'm Mr. M…" His sentence trailed. "Um, Nicky, do you want to ride the train?"

That was all it took to make a fast friend of the young boy, who grabbed the man's hand and pulled him toward the train.

The Phantom scooped Nicky into his arms, placing the boy on his broad shoulders. "Look, there, Nicky! You're as tall as the giraffes, now!"

He was a natural with children, Maddie

thought as they headed for the train, and Nicky was eating up his attention, squealing with glee. Warning bells rang in Maddie's mind, and she quickly installed mental barriers. The more she knew of this man, the more there was to like. But fairy tales didn't translate into reality, and she was setting herself up to be left with a crushed pumpkin and a couple of mice for company.

Something she definitely could do without. She'd have to be more careful.

Maddie's eyes met the Phantom's and he smiled, sharing with her in Nicky's delight. It was a small gesture, yet it warmed her heart like a woodstove on a brisk morning.

"I didn't quite catch your name," she reminded him as he planted Nicky on the train, waving as the locomotive powered up.

A surprised look crossed his face, but was quickly shadowed. "Hmm?" he asked, as if he hadn't heard her question.

"Your *name*. You know, what people call you to get your attention. I can't keep calling you Phantom all the time. It would be embarrassing for me and humiliating for you."

Neil glanced at his watch, stalling for time. He hadn't anticipated seeing her again—or rather, having her see him. And now she was demanding his name.

What was he supposed to say? *Hi, my name is Neil March, the man responsible for your husband's death.*

"I…um," he mumbled, looking right and left, wishing desperately that a gap in the earth would open up and give him an escape route. Swallow him whole. He couldn't tell her the truth, though he knew she deserved to hear it.

"Rory," he said, making a split-second decision. "My friends call me Rory."

It wasn't exactly a lie. He had, in fact, been raised as Rory. Neil Rory March III. His father was already Neil Jr., so adding another Neil to the family clan had seemed a bit confusing. Neil had gone by his middle name until he graduated from college and claimed his inheritance.

"Rory," Maddie repeated, running her low, melodic voice over the syllables. The sound was like a balm to his soul.

"Mrs. Carlton!" The master of ceremonies for the grand opening of the Pachyderm Pavilion rushed upon them, startling Neil. He took a step backward and turned his face away from any who might recognize him. "It's time.

We've been looking all over for you. Everyone is waiting."

A tumult of confusion ensued as Maddie gathered Nicky under her arm and muttered about not noticing the time. Several others in charge of seeing the grand opening go off without a hitch converged on her, giving her instructions on speaking and wishing her luck.

Neil slipped quietly away into the night, away from Maddie, feeling the cold closing around him with every step he took. His hands clenched into fists, trying to force from his mind the lie still ringing in his ears.

My friends call me Rory.

Chapter Five

Keeping to the shadows of the makeshift tent, Neil adjusted the collar of his knee-length wool coat high around his neck. From his pocket he pulled a Colorado Rockies baseball cap, which he placed low over his brow, shadowing his ravaged face from the crowd.

He couldn't afford to have anyone recognize him and uncover his deception.

It was the very same reason that, up until last night, he never went out in public: to keep the world from finding out the truth about that one accursed night. Finding out the truth about *him*.

Until Maddie.

She forced him out of his self-imposed solitude, though she was the last person on earth with whom he wanted to come face-to-face. The irony of his situation cut him like a razor.

He watched her approach the podium nervously, hesitating before the clamoring crowd. From his vantage point near the front and to the right, he could see her hand shaking as she stepped before the microphone. She tapped it gently with her forefinger, then stepped back when the speakers crackled. Neil couldn't help chuckling.

He tamped down the desire to rescue her. She was putting on a good show for the crowd, but he could see the lines of strain around her mouth, the fear shining in her eyes. He wanted to burst forward, take over the situation, put her at ease. He was good with people, had no trouble speaking in public. He could stand by her side, make things easier for her.

But this was her night. As tough as speaking before this crowd was, it was something she needed to do. He couldn't rush in and take her place, not only because it wouldn't be fair to Maddie, but because he'd be recognized. He needed to stay under the cover of darkness.

Clearing her throat, she began again, quietly at first, and then with growing passion, to tell the agonizing story that began and ended with March's Department Store.

She was so beautiful, even with her features

laced with pain and sadness. She looked like an angel from heaven under the stage lights, glowing with a warmth and purity that pervaded even the pain.

Neil's chest tightened. If only it were another place, another time. If he could erase the past, he would be in grave danger of losing his heart.

But the past could never be changed. He would forever live in the cold shadow of Peter Carlton's death.

The chill of the night air enveloped him, the dampness of the light snowfall weighing him down as surely as the guilt burdening his shoulders.

The crowd applauded and Maddie stepped away from the microphone. She grasped Nicky's hand and then wandered through the throng, looking for a familiar face.

Looking for him.

He stepped out of the shadows and turned quickly to leave. He was a coward. His mind berated him even as he walked away. But he couldn't play the game anymore.

He wouldn't. The truth might show in his eyes.

And if she didn't find out…if her big brown eyes met his, he might throw caution to the wind and act on his feelings. He didn't know which was worse. And he didn't want to find out.

He increased his stride and pushed through the crowds, making good his escape.

"Rory, wait!"

She'd seen him. His shoulders stiffened and he slackened his pace. Her words burned inside his chest, but he couldn't help smiling when he looked into her shining eyes. "How did it feel to be up there in front of everyone?" he asked around the guilt clogging his throat.

"I can't believe it. I was so nervous, but once I got up there I just forgot about everything except telling the story. My adrenaline's pumping a mile a minute. It was so…invigorating!"

She reached up and swiped the cap from his head, swatting him playfully in the chest with it.

Neil chuckled and wrenched the cap away from her, tapping her lightly on top of her head before placing the cap in his coat pocket.

With an offended screech, she tried to retrieve it, but he shifted back and forth, always just out of her grasp. "Missed me, Missed me. Now ya gotta kiss me!" he whispered in her ear, hugging her to his chest.

Laughing and sputtering, they both fell into a heap in a cold, wet snowbank. Suddenly her smile faded and self-doubt flooded her expression. "But I— How did I do? Really?"

"You were wonderful, Maddie. Born to be a public speaker."

Maddie grinned. "Now there's hogwash if I've ever heard it. But please—don't stop!" It had been so long since she'd heard a compliment from a man. She felt her cheeks flaming with heat, but she didn't care. Right now she was willing to beg for a compliment from this handsome stranger.

He made her laugh. He made her feel. He made the night light up with thousands of brilliant colors that put the Wildlights to shame.

He pulled her into the curve of his arm, the palm of her hand against his chest. She could feel his heart pounding, and her own heartbeat rose in challenge.

She glanced at her son, hoping the boy was not upset by the sight of this unknown man with his arm around her shoulders. But Nicky seemed oblivious, running ahead with wild abandon from one display to the next. He exclaimed over the lights, bounced excitedly over every new animal he discovered. And when he glanced back at his mother, he only smiled to see her in Rory's arms.

"Shall I tell you how beautiful you are?" Rory whispered as they followed the path her son had taken. "How your brown eyes sparkle in the moonlight?"

"Mmm," Maddie answered, allowing her emotions to be led as her feet were being led. Far from reality and deeply into a dream.

"You can't be serious," she whispered.

"Ah, but I am." He grasped her shoulders and turned her to face him, forcing her to meet his gaze.

"You can feel it," he continued, "here." He placed her palm over his heart. "And you can see it...."

She *could* see into the depths of his blazing dark eyes, see a flicker of untamed emotion so intense that it heated her insides. She couldn't have been married for eight years without recognizing what was happening to her, knowing what she was feeling. Understanding what she'd been missing.

It wasn't just a kiss or a touch that she lacked. She missed the intimacy of two souls meeting, and bonding. She missed this amazing instant and uncanny rapport they shared.

It was what he longed for, as well. She could feel it in her heart. He wasn't playing games with her. The intensity in his eyes left no doubt that he was serious.

And this time, she didn't want to run away.

She knew the moment he read her answer in her eyes. She couldn't have spoken if she had wanted to—except with her heart. And she hoped that was enough for Rory.

He cupped her chin in his palm and shook his head ever so slightly. His dark eyes clouded, but Maddie was beyond being able to do more than lean into him, asking for his affection the only way she could.

"Maddie, I—"

"Rory."

A muffled groan rose from the depths of his chest as he gave in to the longing in his eyes. The unspoken question remained as his gaze locked with hers, and slowly, slowly, he bent his head toward her.

Maddie's senses heightened until she was sure she could feel the crackling of tension in the air between them. His featherlight caress of her cheek, sliding gently to the back of her neck to pull her closer, became the focus of her world.

And those eyes. Those *eyes*.

She wanted to cling to him, to share one breath and heartbeat.

But they both knew this was neither the right time, nor the right place.

Reluctantly, he broke away. "We need to catch up with Nicky," he murmured, and wrapped his arm around her shoulder, holding her so tightly that he could easily have crushed her, yet so gently that she felt surrounded by the strength of a fortress, safe and protected from the fears haunting her.

She closed her eyes, content for the moment to rest her head against his solid shoulder, to extend the shimmering bliss for as long as possible.

Suddenly his muscles tensed beneath her cheek. Her eyes snapped open to see what was wrong, but Rory wasn't looking at her.

Jaw clenched, he scanned the throng of people nearby. "Where'd he go?" he asked. His voice was crisp with authority.

"Nicky?" She pointed toward the predatory-bird display. "Why, he was right over there when—" She stopped midsentence, her eyes searching the area for her son's familiar face. "Where's Nicky?"

He was gone.

Her stomach lurched into her throat. Where was he? He'd been exclaiming over the eagles not a minute before. Before she'd lost herself in Rory's arms.

"Where is he?" she cried, wresting herself from Rory's embrace. "Where's my son? Oh, if anything happens to Nicky…"

"Maddie." Rory's voice was low and controlled.

"I'll never forgive myself. Oh, God, please let him be safe," she prayed aloud.

"Maddie!"

"This was a terrible, terrible mistake. If I hadn't—"

"Maddie!" Rory took her by the shoulders and gently shook her. "You've got to snap out of it. Take some deep breaths and try to calm down. We'll find him."

The even tenor of his words had the needed effect, soothing her soul with steady, reassuring waves. His eyes blazed into hers, transferring his strength to her.

She scrubbed at the tears streaking down her face. "You're right. Let's not panic. He can't be far."

"We need to put this together piece by piece.

A minute ago, Nicky was in front of the eagle cage. Where would he go from there?" Rory took her hand and began backtracking the way they'd come, his eyes alert.

"I don't know!" she wailed, and burst into a fresh round of tears. "He knows not to wander off. He could be anywhere."

"He could be. But he isn't. He's *somewhere*. We've just got to figure out where." His words were firm, almost harsh, but the hand stroking the tears on her cheek was gentle and reassuring.

Maddie strained to think of where her son might be, but she couldn't get past the wild waves of panic in her mind.

She paused as the answer floated just above her consciousness. "The elephants!"

"Didn't he see the elephants earlier?"

"We didn't get a chance. We were too busy with the program. And they've always been his favorite." Her voice caught. "I promised him. And then I was so preoccupied with my stupid speech, and finding you—I forgot all about it."

"Come on, then." He reached for her hand, then sprinted toward the lights of the pavilion, glancing back from time to time to be sure that she was keeping pace.

She was. She held her breath, hoping against hope that her son was safe. The lights from the Pachyderm Pavilion blazed brightly, beckoning visitors. Nicky would have had no trouble finding his way.

Tears streamed from her eyes, though she fought to keep them back. "God, please," she whispered quietly and fervently. "Please. Don't take Nicky, too."

She didn't even realize that she spoke aloud until Rory looked back, his brow furrowed. "He won't," he ground out through clenched teeth. "He can't."

"No?" she yelled, her body quivering with rage. She didn't care that she was making a scene, that others were staring at the couple racing helter-skelter through the zoo. Fury threatened to overwhelm her, and she focused on the anger. It gave her strength. It was easier to be angry than afraid. "Why not? He took Peter."

"Maddie, don't."

Rory's voice was laced with pain, as if her words had been directed toward him. She wasn't angry with him. Rory had distracted her, but only because she let him.

She was mad at herself. And at God.

But most of all at Neil March. It was all *his* fault that she was alone. Neil March was responsible for everything bad that had happened to her—even Nicky's disappearance. If Peter was still alive...

But it wasn't Neil March that she was hurting with her cutting words. It was Rory. Dear, kind Rory, who appeared just as upset by Nicky's disappearance as she was.

She didn't know why it should matter to him, why *she* should matter to him. But somehow she knew that Rory's affection for her and Nicky was real. Her anger subsided, leaving her shoulders in tight knots and her stomach unnervingly empty.

Rory stopped as they reached the pavilion and pulled her to him, his breath coming in short gasps that clouded in the crisp air.

Suddenly his embraced tightened. "Maddie, look. There!"

Chapter Six

A chuckle erupted from Rory's throat.

Maddie looked to where he pointed, then sagged against him in relief. If he hadn't been holding her so tightly, she was certain her legs would have folded beneath her.

Nicky was hanging from the guardrail, leaning as far as his gangly body would let him, straining to touch a friendly elephant's trunk. He was talking animatedly to the beast, and didn't even seem to notice that he'd left his mother far behind.

He's growing up, Maddie thought, the realization pinching her heart. But she knew that Nicky would indeed have panicked once he lost interest in the elephants and realized that he was alone.

Just as she and every other child, at some

point in their young lives, had done. She remembered the shocking revelation in her own life—that she was nothing more than a tiny dot on the huge map of civilization. And that she was totally and completely alone.

She'd been shopping in a department store with her father, and begging to be able to stop and look at a colorful rack of books. Her father, thinking he'd give his daughter a moment to browse, had stepped two aisles over to look at hand tools—well within earshot, but completely out of Maddie's sight.

How she'd screamed, her little heart frantic. She'd been completely terrified.

And had felt utterly alone.

It had happened again when Peter died, and then again for this brief period when she thought she'd lost Nicky. Fortunately, she'd found him before he'd suffered any trauma over the incident. In fact, she was relatively positive he didn't even know there had *been* an incident.

If only her own heart was so strong.

"Thank God we found him," Rory said, echoing the silent prayer in her own thoughts.

He marched up to the boy and picked him off

the rail by the waist. Nicky yelled and squirmed, but Rory held him tightly until he'd calmed.

"You little scamp!" he chastised gently but firmly. "You gave your mother and me a healthy scare."

Nicky started to protest, then looked at Maddie. She knew she couldn't hide her tear-streaked face, and a fresh wave of tears already threatened to engulf her.

"Young man!" she said in her best mother's voice. "Don't you *ever* wander off on me again. Is that understood?"

Nicky's bottom lip quivered endearingly. Maddie gave him a moment, then opened her arms to him. He dashed to her, and she held him tight, squeezing her eyes tight against the tears. Her dear little man. And he was safe. *Thank You, God,* she silently prayed. *Forgive me for my anger. I know I should have trusted You.*

"I'm okay, Mom," Nicky assured, wiggling out of her embrace. "I got kinda lost, but an old lady helped me find the elephants. She told me to stay here till you got here. And she helped me feed that big guy in the middle!"

Maddie touched his shoulder, reassuring herself once again that he was here. He was safe.

"I think we could all use a nice hot cup of cocoa," Rory said, lightly embracing both Maddie and her son. "What do you say we head up to the front gate? There's a restaurant where we can get in out of the cold for a bit." He ruffled Nicky's hair. "I think it's called Elephant something."

"Cool!" Nicky exclaimed, undaunted by his near-trauma.

Smiling at her son's enthusiasm, Maddie agreed, and moments later the three of them were settled in a cozy corner booth with steaming mugs of whipped-cream-topped cocoa.

Neil stared at Maddie, trying to memorize every line and plane of her delicately beautiful face. He was living a precious dream, just being with her, but he knew the night would soon end.

And though it tore him inside to acknowledge it, there wouldn't be any more nights with Maddie. There couldn't be. He was her worst nightmare come to life, worse by far than the Phantom he'd been when he first met her.

If only she knew.

Maddie picked up her mug and toasted. "To happy endings."

Neil's breath caught in his throat. He couldn't speak. Instead, he lifted his own mug and nodded.

She took a tentative sip of the cocoa, then licked at the whipped cream on top, not realizing that a small dollop of cream dotted her nose.

Neil smiled and leaned toward her, wiping off the cream with the tip of his finger. The brief contact was electric. Their eyes met and held.

His hand traveled lightly down her arm until he'd reached her fingers, which he laced through his own. "You're trembling," he murmured.

Maddie pulled back and crossed her arms. She looked away and took a deep breath, then looked back at him. "I'm just so *angry*."

"Do you want to talk about it?"

She shook her head, then appeared to think better of it. She put an arm around Nicky's shoulders and gave him a squeeze. "Son, since you're done with your cocoa, why don't you go play with those toys over in the Kids' Corner?" She gestured to a corner full of stuffed animals and building blocks. "I think I see an elephant."

Nicky's eyes brightened, and he scrambled over his mother to make a beeline for the toys.

Maddie blew out a breath, squared her shoulders, and locked eyes with Neil's. "Yeah. I do want to talk about it."

Neil nodded.

"I can't help it. I know God wants me to forgive him, and I've tried and tried, but then something like this happens and I get mad all over again."

"Who are you angry at?" He braced himself for the answer he already knew.

"Neil March."

He hadn't prepared well enough to shield himself from hearing his own name thrown like a javelin. To hear his condemnation from her own mouth was almost more than he could bear. Then again, maybe he deserved the pain he was feeling.

"Why?" He croaked the word from a dry mouth, then sought solace in the dregs of his mug. The bitter chocolate taste was fitting, somehow.

"It's his fault I'm in this predicament." She took a deep breath and clasped her mug with whitened knuckles. "I've…never told anyone this before. I don't know if…"

"You don't have to tell me," Neil murmured, relieved by the reprieve she offered.

She looked him in the eye and smiled wearily. "I believe I do. I've been carrying this around with me so long that I... I just want to share it with someone. Do you mind?" Tentatively, she reached for his hand.

Neil's chest constricted until he thought his heart would burst. "No." He forced the words from reluctant lips. "Of course I don't mind."

"Peter and I—" she looked away "—we were having...problems. I... He... We weren't the happy couple we appeared to be. I think he..."

She stopped, her face crumpling with pain.

"You think he...?" Neil prompted gently.

Maddie straightened her shoulders and met his eyes. "I think he was going to leave me. For another woman."

Neil shut his eyes and gulped for air, unable to stand the swirls of pain clouding her eyes. How could a man even consider leaving Maddie? He knew enough about her to know she would be devoted to her marriage, as she was devoted to her child. A wave of anger rose in Neil. Anger at Peter Carlton for hurting Maddie.

His desire to protect her surprised him, and he fought to keep astonishment from registering on his face.

For the first time in his life, he was looking beyond himself, wondering what sharing his life with another person would be like. Maddie wasn't like the glitz-and-glamour women he was accustomed to.

He could fall in love with a woman like Maddie. She sparked powerful feelings in him—feelings that started the first time he saw her, the first time he held her in his arms. And every moment since then—with every look, every touch—the feeling had grown deeper. Stronger.

For all the good it did him. God must have a strange sense of humor, for Neil could never act on his feelings. *Never.*

"What does this have to do with Neil March?" he asked after a lengthy silence.

"Nothing. And everything. Peter and I were fighting, as usual. He took Nicky in to look at the Santa's workshop display to get away from me. I was furious. I was going to—" She paused. "I felt like walking out of that store and just walking, as far away from him as I could. I…wasn't even going to take Nicky. I can't even imagine how I—"

A sob escaped her throat, and she clapped a

hand over her mouth to stifle any further display of emotion.

After taking a moment to regain her composure, she continued. "Suddenly, the whole thing went up in flames. It was so fast. So final."

She paused and swiped a hand down her face. "Someone ran into the fire and rescued Nicky, but it was too late for Peter."

"That must have been terrible for you." He squeezed her hand, wishing with all his heart that he could take her in his arms and shield her from any more hurt.

"We never got a chance to make up. We were *fighting* when he died. I think I could have handled it better if he *had* left me for another woman. But this way…nothing's resolved."

"And until it is, you can't go on with your own life?"

"Yes, I suppose that's true. But what can I do? I'm a prisoner of the past, unable to resolve my feelings, to accept what I must and move on."

"That's not true," Neil denied.

Maddie snorted. "No? Then why am I in such bad shape after a year? You'd think I could at least talk about it."

"You *are* talking about it. And a year isn't so very long to grieve."

"Is that what you call it? Grieving? I don't think I've got to grieving yet. I'm still too angry."

"At Neil." It wasn't a question, and Neil braced himself for the answer.

"At Neil. I've heard about him, you know."

Neil laughed without mirth. "What have you heard?"

"He's a playboy. An arrogant rich kid with more money than brains. Proved it, too, after Peter died."

"How so?" He could almost hear the heavy thud of another block of guilt dropping onto his already burdened shoulders. Every word she spoke, every pained glance, added further weight to the millstone dragging him down.

The only thing that kept him from bolting from the table was the knowledge that he deserved her words, and more. He had no defense. He was guilty as charged on all counts.

"By sending me that money. As if money could right the wrong. Erase the past and tie everything up in a neat little bow." Her voice raised an octave. "Well, it doesn't work that way. And sometimes I wish I could tell Mr. High-and-Mighty Neil March that to his face."

You just have, Neil thought, taking a deep breath to steady his nerves. The only thing that kept him from laughing bitterly was the knowledge that such an exclamation would give his masquerade away. He felt like tipping the table, thrusting his fist through the glass window through which he stared into the darkness of night. "You've never seen Neil March, have you?"

"No. And frankly, I don't want to. I'd probably spit in his face. It's blood money, that's what it is. A guilt offering."

Blood money. The accusation rang in his ears, temporarily blinding him with its intensity. And its truth.

It *was* blood money. Because he could do no less. And because he could do no more. Though he wished with all his heart and soul that he could trade places with the dead man. Give Peter back to her.

Peter didn't deserve her, but Maddie was suffering so. Neil felt that he would do anything to relieve her pain. Pain she didn't ask for, and shouldn't have had.

If only he could.

Neil attempted a smile. A pathetic attempt, he thought, wondering if she could see his lips quivering with effort. "Aren't you afraid you're going to run into Neil March now that you are out in society?"

"I'm *not* out in society. The masquerade ball was a fluke. The only reason I went is because it was a benefit for Children's Hospital."

That was the reason he had gone, too. He tightened his lips to a straight line to keep himself from frowning.

"Nicky suffered severe smoke inhalation through that fire. Thank God he wasn't burned. Children's Hospital got him through it."

"Thank God," Neil murmured, and squeezed her hand.

"Yes. I don't think I would have made it if God had taken Nicky, too. That's why I panicked tonight."

He glanced toward the Kids' Corner, where Nicky was playing with large, stuffed zoo animals. Something clinched his heart at the sight of the happy young boy whose life had been spared.

"As for Neil March," Maddie continued, drawing his attention back to her face, "I'll admit the thought crossed my mind that I might run into him at the ball. Fortunately, I didn't. And I'm sure he would never dare show his miserable hide here."

Neil shook his head.

"He knows I'm the major benefactor for this event. How could he not? It's his money I'm spending. But it would take a much bigger man than Neil March to face me down—to come to terms with what he's done."

"You're probably right." Neil ran a finger around the top of his empty mug. His thoughts were racing, and guilt stabbed at his soul.

It would take a much bigger man than Neil March to face me down—to come to terms with what he's done.

It was true. Neil rued the day he was born, but there was no way he would ever come to terms with what he'd done.

And now he'd gone and made things worse. He should have ripped his mask off the moment Maddie had revealed her identity that night on the carriage. He should have declared his name, taken responsibility for his actions right there and then. Apologized and begged her forgiveness.

He should have…

But it was too late for that. He'd wound his

web of lies so tightly around himself that he couldn't escape even if he wanted to.

How was he going to tell her now? How could he explain why, after discovering her identity, he had purposefully sought her out again. How he had concealed his identity, even when she mentioned his name. How he'd spent not one, but *two* evenings with her—all the while knowing that he was the bane of her existence. He'd deceived her, when all she deserved was kindness, love and truth.

If she found out now, she would despise him even more, if that were possible. Could he find the strength to tell her the truth? To face the consequences?

He had to find that strength. Maddie deserved the truth. And he deserved to suffer alone with his guilty burden and the memory of the hatred in her eyes when she spoke his name.

"Do you not want to talk about it?"

"What?" Neil asked vaguely, his mind still turning over the possibilities.

"I asked," Maddie said gently, meeting his eyes, "what happened to your face. But if you don't want to talk about it, I'll understand."

Rory had grown so silent that she wondered if she had hit a sore spot with him.

His looks didn't matter to her. Not with his kind heart and gentle ways. But that was beside the point, for he was strikingly handsome on the side of his face she could see.

Whatever he was hiding...whatever sort of scar marred the right side of his face, could only intensify the almost ethereal beauty of his countenance. His dark complexion and angular features would only be enhanced by a scar, making him appear even more rugged and virile.

"It doesn't matter to me," she whispered, reaching up to stroke the bandage with the tip of her finger. "I was just curious."

Rory's eyes clouded and he looked away. She had obviously touched a nerve, and she regretted the impulse that had made her ask.

She floundered for a way to redeem herself, stuttering to several false starts while Rory stared moodily out the window.

After several minutes of silence, he said, "I think we should go."

His voice was so gruff, so angry. Everything was falling apart, and she hadn't the slightest idea how to fix it. Oh, *why* had she opened her big mouth?

"Oh. Okay," she said finally, removing her hand from his grasp and clutching her purse. "We can leave. Let me get Nicky bundled up and we're out of here."

Rory nodded vaguely and continued staring out the window.

"Rory, would you mind walking me out to my car? I don't like walking alone in a parking lot this late at night." It sounded juvenile to her own ears, but she was desperate, grasping for anything that might keep her in his company for a few minutes longer. At least until she could find a way to straighten out the mess she'd created, bring a smile back to his handsome face.

"Hmm? Sure." Rory called Nicky over and helped her with the boy's coat, hat and mittens. He thrust a baseball cap on his own head and pulled the brim low over his brow.

He held the door for her, then walked off ahead of her, his collar up against the wind and his hands stuffed deeply in the pockets of his coat. Like a man who didn't want to be disturbed, Maddie thought.

He was going to leave her again, just the

way he had the night before. Without a word. Without a trace. Without any way for her to discover his last name. She knew it with a certainty that permeated her entire being.

And she was just as certain that she couldn't let that happen.

"Rory, wait!" she called, rushing to his side.

He turned, a gentle smile on his lips.

She wasn't sure what she'd say when she reached him; she only knew that she had to try. His smile erased her fear, gave her courage to continue.

Until she had met Rory, she had expected to spend the rest of her life alone. But now, looking into the eyes of this kind, gentle man, sharing small moments of joy with him, she was starting to think she could recover from the wounds she nursed. Her Phantom might not be the man she could share the rest of her life with, but he was a beginning.

"I want to see you again," she blurted out before she lost her nerve. She placed an imploring hand on his sleeve, her eyes begging him not to leave, not to run out on her again.

His jaw tightened and he looked away.

Rejecting her in the kindest way he knew, she thought. Her throat tightened until she thought she would choke. She coughed for a breath, then whirled around and walked away, trying to keep her steps slow and even, trying not to reveal how deeply his silent rebuff had hurt her.

"Come on, Nicky, let's go!" she said harshly, turning to see if her son followed.

"Maddie." Rory was at her side, matching his pace to hers. He wouldn't look at her, even now.

"I'm sorry," she muttered. "I'm not usually so forward. It's just that I thought... Well, it doesn't matter what I thought. Forget I said anything."

"No," her Phantom said firmly, engulfing her small hand in his. His voice sounded strained and unnaturally deep. "Don't apologize."

They walked in silence for a moment, their fingers laced. Maddie tried to still her heart at his touch, tried not to hope that he had changed his mind.

Suddenly he stopped and turned her by the shoulders to face him. "More than anything in this world, I want to see you again. It's just that you don't know—"

"What you look like?" Maddie interrupted.

"That doesn't matter to me. You're a good man. It's what's inside that counts."

Rory laughed, but his smile didn't reach his dark, clouded eyes. "Thanks for the vote of confidence, but that wasn't what I was going to say. I—"

A group of reporters appeared as if from nowhere, shining lights in their eyes and thrusting microphones at their mouths.

"Mrs. Carlton, do you plan to…"

"Is this man your new significant other?"

"And you, sir…"

"Of all the—" he began, a hunted look in his eyes. He pushed the microphones away, pulled his cap even lower over his eyes.

"Mrs. Carlton, do you plan to remarry?" A pale, wide-eyed woman concluded her sentence with several thrusts of the tip of her pencil.

Maddie batted it away and flashed Rory a beseeching look. *Get us out of here!* she begged with her gaze.

Rory elbowed his way forward until he was able to slip a stabilizing hand around Maddie's waist. She breathed a sigh of relief as he leaned his head toward hers.

"Maddie, I've got to go," he whispered

coarsely in her ear. "Come to the Parade of Lights. I'll find you."

She stiffened. Instead of rescuing her from this swarm of poisonous media personnel, he was leaving. Again. And without her.

A particularly aggressive young man grabbed the sleeve of her jacket and whirled her around, thrusting a microphone under her chin.

"If you would care to comment on—"

Rory! She wrenched her arm from the reporter's grasp and held out her hands to Rory. He had to stay. She hadn't even asked him his last name!

With an apologetic shake of his head he stepped forward, taking her by the shoulders and sweeping a gentle kiss across her cheek. And then he was gone, pushing his way through the cameras with his head bent low.

"Wait!" Maddie called, but he had already disappeared.

"Mrs. Carlton? Can you please tell us why you…"

Maddie put her arm around Nicky and guided him away from the reporters, following the path Rory had taken. She couldn't deal with reporters, not when her heart was rocking harder than a ship in a storm.

Why had the reporters scared him away? Was he so afraid of revealing his scars that he had to run and hide? Reporters were fast becoming a natural, if annoying, part of her life. But she wanted *Rory* to be a part of her life, too.

"I don't even know your last name. How will I find you?" she whispered into the biting night air.

Come to the Parade of Lights. I'll find you.

His words echoed in her mind. She didn't know how Rory would pick her out of the crowd, but deep in her heart she knew it would happen.

Somehow, someway, her Phantom would find her.

Chapter Seven

Maddie sighed in relief as she pulled off the two-lane highway into the small, eastern town of Benton, Colorado. She didn't make the trip as often as she should, she thought with a stab of guilt. Her mother, Celia, and her stepfather, Davis, were only a three-hour drive from Denver.

Nicky would have wanted to be with her today, but she purposely picked a time when he was in school, so she could spend some time alone with her mother.

As for her son's disappointment when he discovered what he'd missed, she promised herself she'd make it up to him, maybe take him up for a visit during his Christmas vacation.

She had more important things to worry

about. Like what to do about Rory. He made her heart feel things she was sure she'd never feel again. How could a person be elated with joy and scared to death at the same time? But that's what Rory did to her.

But was she ready for a relationship?

When she was with Rory, the question seemed to answer itself. It felt so natural to be around him, to confide in him, to melt into his embrace. He made her laugh, and feel the sheer joy of being alive again. The sensation even clung for a few extra hours, hovering around Maddie like a warm, welcome cocoon. But by the next morning, back came all the fears and doubts.

And guilt. She gripped the steering wheel with her fist, easing into the slower, small-town traffic. How could she go on with her life when Peter was still hovering in the corner of her thoughts? With nothing resolved, it was difficult to consider moving on.

And even if she could put her past with Peter to rest, there was still Nicky. The boy seemed to like Rory, but there was a gigantic chasm of difference between liking a man who took him riding on the zoo train and accepting a man who consistently took his mother's time and stole away some of her attentiveness—attention Nicky was used to having for himself.

She pulled into the driveway of her mother's ranch-style house and shut down the engine, but didn't make a move to open the door. Instead she sat staring at the friendly redbrick exterior of the house, remembering her own happy childhood there.

She'd learned to roller-skate and bicycle on this driveway. She'd pinched her fingers in the front door. She'd helped her mother plant the now-hibernating rosebushes that lined the front of the house.

She'd experienced her first kiss on the front-porch swing, had her prom pictures taken under the towering maple tree.

Maddie smiled wistfully. She'd had a wonderful, happy childhood here in this home. At least until her father had run out on her mother and her.

She pulled the key from the ignition and tossed it in her purse. She was surprised at how much her father's leaving still hurt. But having a parent desert you when you were twelve—a blossom just beginning to open and flower—wasn't something you ever got over. Not completely.

She could picture the scene as if it were yesterday, her mother down on her knees at the bedside, clutching a hastily scrawled note in her hand. Celia's red-rimmed eyes had filled with compassion as she embraced her only daughter and quietly spoke the words that changed Maddie's world.

He's gone, Maddie. Your father's not coming back.

No explanation. No excuse. Just goodbye.

Maddie didn't know how her mother had survived. Celia was the strongest, most resilient person Maddie knew. Her faith in the goodness of God never wavered, not even when she was faced with raising a child alone in a society not yet ready to accept single mothers.

No one blinked an eye at the fact that Maddie was raising Nicky alone, but Maddie knew her mother hadn't been so lucky. In a small town like Benton, news traveled fast, and opinions, once formed, were difficult to alter. People had turned their backs on the abandoned mother and child.

She could still remember overhearing people speak in low tones about "that woman," as if her mother had done something to run her father out of town. In some bizarre, twisted way, Paul Myers's desertion had fallen squarely on Celia's shoulders.

But Celia had just smiled and continued to think the best of people, starting her own greenhouse to provide for her daughter. No one in Benton would buy anything from her, but there were plenty of vendors in Denver anxious to purchase her mother's hothouse plants. Between working her greenhouse in the daytime and waitressing at night, Celia made enough for both of them to live comfortably and put a little aside for the future. It was Celia's strongest wish that her daughter attend college, have the opportunity to go beyond herself, to be a part of something bigger.

And then Davis Winthrow entered their lives, throwing a man-size wrench into their plans. Her mother had welcomed Davis's commitment and love. Maddie had hated it. Hated *him*. She was too old to favor a replacement father, and why should she want one anyway? No one, most especially Davis Winthrow, could convince her otherwise.

From a twelve-year-old's limited viewpoint, Davis was stealing her mother's love—attention Maddie coveted. She couldn't see that

Davis made her mother happy, didn't understand that the human heart could expand to give limitless love to all it embraced.

In her mind, she'd been replaced, removed from Celia's heart to make room for Davis. She'd been hurt, but mostly she'd been angry. And she'd spent the next six years doing her best to make Davis regret marrying her mother.

She slammed her hands hard against the steering wheel. No way would she do that to Nicky. She wasn't about to risk losing him to a love that might well be all in her mind. She wouldn't make the same mistake Celia had, however well-intended her mother's actions had been. But she didn't want to give Rory up, either, which left her at an impasse—a gap impossible to bridge.

Unless her mother could help her work things out. She let herself out of the car and went around the side of the house, through a picket-fence gate and into the backyard, to the hand-built hothouse where she knew her mother would be.

"Mom?" Her call echoed into the steamy, sunshine-filled room.

"Madelaine?" Her mother sounded surprised, sending another tiny dart of guilt into

Maddie's chest. Celia Winthrow, pleasantly plump from years of home cooking, stepped from behind a potted palm, brushing fresh soil from her hands.

Maddie gave her mother a hug, and they both retreated to the house. The tiny country kitchen smelled of fresh-baked chocolate-chip cookies, Maddie's favorite.

Her mother washed the dirt from her hands, then set a tray of cookies in front of Maddie and poured two tall glasses of milk. Maddie chuckled at the old-fashioned gesture that was so much her mother.

"What's wrong?" Celia asked, scooting a chair close to Maddie's and sneaking a cookie for herself.

"I didn't say anything was wrong," Maddie protested, also biting into one of the delightfully sweet cookies. "I didn't even say hello yet."

"Hello to you, too. But you don't come all the way to Benton to say hello."

Maddie grimaced. "You've got me there. I'm sorry, Mom. It's been a rough year."

"It has," her mother agreed, patting her on the hand. "But you'll never be a burden to me, you know."

"I know." Maddie went silent as she considered what to say. Four hours ago it had seemed like the only alternative: seeking her mother's advice. But now she didn't know how to begin, what to say. Her mother and stepfather had loved Peter. He'd healed the breach in their family, made things right again.

Whatever Maddie's doubts, her fears about their marriage, Peter had been a Godsend to her family. And now he was gone.

And Maddie was floundering. Her parents loved Peter like a son. His peacemaking shoes were impossible to fill. She wasn't about to tell Celia that she suspected Peter of cheating on her, that she believed he was about to desert Maddie as Paul Myers had once deserted Celia. It would break her mother's heart, a heart that had suffered more than a lifetime's worth of pain.

No, Peter's memory was going to remain sparkling white and pure as a gentle smile. He would continue to remain the son her mother never had.

She felt a quiver of dismay creep up her back as she considered telling them about Rory. How would Celia take to hearing about a new man in Maddie's life?

"Best way is just to spit it out." Celia reached for another cookie.

Maddie sighed. "Do you remember how it felt when you... How did you meet Davis?"

"Davis?" Her mother's white eyebrows rose and her cheeks colored a pleasant pink. "Why, he came into the restaurant where I was waitressing."

"And?" Celia's cheeks went from pink to a fiery red. Her mother was actually blushing! Maddie couldn't remember ever having seen that before.

"He said I poured the meanest cup of coffee he'd ever seen, and would I go out to a movie with him."

Maddie pressed down the distrust that talking about Davis aroused. Years of fighting with the man, of disliking him because of his place in her mother's life, was hard to ignore. Her chest filled with anger.

You're acting like a pigheaded, stubborn teenager! Peter's voice rang in her ears as if he sat on her shoulder—her nagging conscience. *Davis Winthrow has reached out to you every way he knows how. Now it's up to you to do the reaching.*

"How did you feel?" she asked at last, trying

to put a damper on her emotions. She must be overtired, she decided, for her mood to be fluctuating so drastically. She and Davis had been getting along for years now. Her initial reaction had to be the result of being stressed out.

"Flattered." Celia bit into her cookie and washed the bite down with milk. "Maddie, what are we talking about here?"

"Me." Maddie sighed again and met her mother's kind, pale eyes. "I've…met someone."

Her mother squeezed her hand. "Maddie, that's wonderful!"

"It is?" Whatever she had imagined her mother's reaction to be—reserve, distrust, antagonism—this wasn't it. There was joy radiating from her mother's face.

"Yes, ma'am, it is! This is Hallelujah and dance-on-the-tables news, and make no mistaking!"

"I thought you'd be…upset," Maddie admitted, smiling in spite of herself. Celia was literally bouncing in her chair, looking as if she might well act on her words and bound onto the table.

"Upset? Why would I be…?"

Maddie grimaced.

"Peter was a good man, Maddie." Celia nodded her understanding. "But he's gone. And you've got a lot of living left to do. I'm *glad* you're ready to move on."

Peter was a good man. Maddie's heart twisted. She wished with all her heart she could believe that, and remember only the good times with Peter. But there were too many unanswered questions for her to rest easy on that score. "I don't *feel* ready. Because—"

"Because Peter's memory keeps lurking in the back of your mind."

Maddie bit the edge of her lip and nodded. "I don't want to sound like I'm whining or complaining. I've hibernated for a year doing just that—feeling sorry for myself and refusing to acknowledge that I have a life beyond what I had with Peter."

"He'd want you to be happy, you know."

"I know. Everyone keeps telling me that, but it seems like a pat answer. I feel so awkward, like a baby just learning to walk."

"Or like an adult trying to learn to walk again after being paralyzed? That's what's happened to you, you know."

Paralyzed. That's exactly how her heart had felt until Rory had set it back in motion. "How did you get over—" Maddie cleared her throat, trying to force the last word from her lips "—Daddy?"

Celia's eyes clouded with pain, and Maddie regretted the impulsive question, however important the answer was.

"I didn't *get over* him."

Celia's answer rocked Maddie to the core of her soul. How could her mother harbor feelings for a man who'd abandoned her?

"Paul was my first love, as Peter is to you. Yes, Paul deserted me. I struggle with a sense of anger and betrayal to this day on that account. But whatever his faults, I loved Paul, and that love will always be part of me."

Whatever his faults. A cold knot formed in Maddie's stomach and began churning.

"It took me a long time, but I forgave your father for running out on us, and forgave myself, as well. I felt like a complete fool, falling in love with a man who didn't care enough for me to stick around through the hard times. I was angry at myself for misjudging him, for trusting him. I might as well have branded the word *stupid* on my forehead for all to see."

She paused and took a sip of milk. "I had to accept myself. And my love for Paul. It was the only way I could clear my mind, release the hate and anger, and learn to love again."

Maddie wanted to comfort her mother, to apologize for reopening old wounds, unearthing emotions best left buried in the past. Instead, it was Celia reaching out a comforting hand to Maddie.

"You don't need to feel guilty about loving Peter," she whispered, stroking her daughter's temple with the back of her hand. "The amazing thing about the human heart is that there is always room for more love. You don't have to replace one love with another. You don't have to abandon your feelings for Peter to move on with your life. I love Davis with all my heart, but in a different way from the way I loved Paul."

Yes. That's how it was with Rory. Her feelings for Rory were as different from her feelings for Peter as black from white. But they weren't any less real, any less powerful, for being different.

When her mother explained it, everything made sense. The puzzle pieces slid into place. If she and Peter hadn't been fighting…

And then there was Nicky. "I hated Davis

for taking you away from me," she blurted, then clapped a hand over her mouth in dismay.

Celia just chuckled. "Don't I know it. You made his life pretty miserable for a few years."

Maddie winced. "Think he'll ever forgive me?"

"He loves you. He always has."

"I guess I knew that." Maddie swallowed hard. "I was wrong. But that doesn't change the way it was for me—for us. How can I do the same thing to Nicky?"

"Your circumstances are different," Celia gently reminded. "Nicky is only six. He needs a father figure, be it the man you've met, or someone else." She patted her palm against her ample bosom. "I know in my heart you weren't meant to be alone, Maddie. You are a beautiful woman both inside and out. And I'm not the least bit surprised that a nice young man has noticed. Don't keep your life on hold any longer."

"But Nicky—"

"Nicky will adjust. And he'll be happier because *you* are happier. Peter didn't leave you, Maddie. He didn't make a choice to walk out the door and never return. He was nothing at all like your father."

Wasn't he? Maddie didn't know. Those last moments were a blur. But her mother was right in one regard: Peter didn't choose to die. Whether or not he *would* have left her was another question, one to which Maddie didn't have an answer. She wasn't even sure she *wanted* an answer. Maybe she was better off not knowing.

"What's his name, dear?"

"Hmm?" Maddie stopped twirling the cookie on her plate and met her mother's kind gaze. "Oh. Sorry. I was zoning out. His name is Rory."

"Rory what?"

Maddie felt her cheeks warm. She should have known her mother would ask. "I don't know," she reluctantly admitted. "I've never been able to wriggle it out of him."

"Sounds intriguing." Her mother laughed.

"Intriguing. And exasperating." Maddie blew out a labored breath. "Frankly, I'm scared to death. Not of Rory. He seems a gem. But having a relationship after Peter…"

Her mother's face drew closed, her eyes sobered and her brow puckered. "I remember—" she sighed "—all too well. You don't feel right with another man, but you don't feel right without him."

"Exactly." Maddie closed her eyes, savoring the wave of relief that washed through her. Somehow, just knowing that her mother understood, and had been through something similar to what Maddie was facing, helped more than a bookshelf full of advice.

Been there. Done that. Bought the T-shirt. Maybe she wasn't crazy, after all. And maybe things would work out between her and Rory.

"It will get easier," Celia said as if reading her thoughts. "Don't rush it. But don't run from it, either. Enjoy your mystery man for today, and let tomorrow take care of itself. That's what The Good Book says to do."

"Loosely translated by Mom," Maddie said with a grin.

"What'd Mom do now?" Davis asked, entering the kitchen and leaning over Maddie's shoulder to snatch a handful of cookies. He welcomed Maddie, ruffling her hair affectionately, then leaned his thick shoulder against the door frame.

Davis Winthrow was a handsome, barrelchested man in his late fifties, with hair as black as the day he'd first walked into their lives, albeit a little thinner on top. His brown eyes twinkled with merriment as he winked at his stepdaughter.

Maddie forced herself to relax under his friendly gaze. Anger had no place in their relationship now.

It wouldn't take a genius to know Davis was a good man, and that he loved her mother to distraction. Maddie couldn't deny it. She didn't even want to.

But it was still hard. Hard to trust. Hard to love.

She turned her smile on Davis. "Mom's just giving me some words of wisdom."

Davis rolled his eyes. "Quotin' Scripture at you again, eh, Maddie? Now you know what I have to put up with," he teased, his gaze pausing for one loving second on Celia's profile.

Maddie couldn't help but smile.

"Oh, sit down, you big oaf!" Celia bantered, winking at Maddie. "And you can get your own milk."

"It's okay," said Maddie with a laugh. "Advice is what I came for."

"Brave woman," Davis muttered before he ducked under the wet tea towel Celia pelted at him.

Maddie laughed again and reached for another

cookie. This was the most comfortable she'd felt around her mom—around her parents—in many years. Even when Peter was around, she couldn't quite lift the burden of hurt from her shoulders. But now, for once, she felt relaxed, at home in the house she'd grown up in.

Celia lifted a questioning eyebrow at Maddie. She wouldn't say a word without Maddie's consent.

Maddie felt her face flush with heat, feeling like a teenager getting ready for her first date. Well, she wasn't a teenager anymore, however awkward she felt. She nodded slightly. "You can tell him."

"She's met a young man," Celia informed Davis, a sparkle in her eye.

"That so?" He stroked a hand down his chin and pinched one eye closed. "And when do we get to meet this here feller?"

Maddie rolled her eyes at Davis's put-on country speech. He was a small-town man, but not a hillbilly. "I don't even know if *I'm* going to see him again."

"Why not?" Celia rolled a finger through one of the curls set in her snow-white hair.

"She's just afraid I'll scare him off," Davis grunted.

"You couldn't scare a fly, ya ol' fool. Maddie, dear, what's wrong?"

Maddie quickly wiped away the traces of tears that sprang to her eyes.

The animosity she'd once felt toward Davis was gone and with it the heavy burden of guilt she carried. She'd been unfair to him when she'd accused him of stealing her mother's affection from her. He'd wanted to add his in. Why had it taken her this long to realize what a good man he was, how happy he made her mother?

And he'd never held it against her. She sighed, half in regret, half in shame.

Nothing was wrong, for a change. She felt like laughing and crying and singing, all at once. She squeezed her eyes tightly shut, savoring the refreshing jumble of feelings.

When she opened her eyes, it was to two perplexed, if humor-laced, stares.

"What?" she asked, stifling a giggle.

"You okay?" Davis queried.

"Fine. Never been better."

Celia smiled, then giggled along with her daughter.

Davis grunted and rolled his eyes. "Females.

Cry when they're distressed, cry when they're angry, cry when they're happy. Go figure."

Maddie hugged Davis and her mother close, and they all burst into happy laughter.

Neil winced as the cold steel of the surgeon's scissors slid against the tender flesh of his cheek.

The doctor paused.

"Do it," Neil grumbled, closing his eyes and forcing the muscles in his shoulders to slacken. "Just do it."

However loose his shoulder muscles were, he knew he wasn't fooling Doc Ryan. His white-knuckled grip on the armrests of the medical chair was a red flag.

Doc Ryan patted him on the shoulder. "This shouldn't hurt, Neil. Your wounds are fully healed."

Neil grunted noncommittally.

"Of course, you can always elect further reconstructive surgery if what we've done here isn't enough for you."

"Just get the bandage off," Neil barked, then flinched at the unnecessarily rough tenor of his voice. It wasn't Doc's fault that he had these scars.

Today would be the first time in over a year

that he would see his face without a bandage. The thought wasn't cheerful.

"There, now," Doc said, removing the last of the bandages. "That wasn't so bad, now, was it, son?"

Neil shook his head, then reached up to touch the unusually soft, puckered skin around his right temple. It felt like the skin of a newborn baby. He clenched his teeth as his gut twisted and turned.

"Look bad, Doc?"

Doc Ryan set his hands on his hips, pursed his lips and raised one gray, bushy eyebrow. "Nah," he said after a short perusal. "I've seen a lot worse mugs than yours, and they ain't been through the trauma you've seen."

"Yeah?" Neil asked, unable to keep relief from flooding into his voice. Life as a deformed man hadn't bothered him a month ago. Now he wished with all his heart that his scars—both those his reflection would reveal and those buried deep in his soul—would disappear. For Maddie. *Because* of Maddie.

"Yeah," Doc Ryan said firmly. "You've still got a scar, and no mistaking. But hey, ladies go for them rough-and-tough, mysterious men.

More of a mark of distinction than a scar, really."

Neil chuckled. There was only one lady he wanted to impress, and he wasn't nearly as confident as was Doc Ryan that she would look on his scar in a positive light.

Especially once she knew the truth.

But Maddie definitely liked mysterious men. She'd been attracted to his Phantom's mask. At least he had that in his favor. For now.

"So can I see it?" His voice was a good octave lower than normal, and he paused to clear his throat and run a hand across the stubble on his jawline.

"Of course." Doc Ryan passed him a handheld mirror. "Not the best image, I'm afraid, but it'll give you a general idea how you look."

Neil held his breath as he raised the mirror to eye level. He forced himself to keep his face neutral, his eyes open, to remain steady no matter what he saw in the mirror.

He breathed a sigh of relief as he realized it wasn't some deformed beast staring back at him. It was his own countenance, the face that had graced countless newspaper advertisements before the accident.

He drew the mirror closer and peered anxiously at his right temple. The skin was lighter, and pulled slightly around the faint outline of his scar. A single finger of scarred flesh trailed down his cheek, nipping into his five-o'clock shadow.

Setting the mirror on a nearby tray, he rubbed his palms across his knees. "Not bad, Doc. Not bad at all."

"I'm glad you think so," Doc said wryly. "I wouldn't want my best customer to think I'd done a shoddy job on him. Bad for business."

"Harrumph." Neil shook his head. "With what you charge, you can live for a year off one patient."

Doc Ryan crossed his arms over his chest. "And I'm well worth every penny," he countered with a grin.

"That you are," Neil agreed easily. "Wouldn't find me saying otherwise."

Doc rubbed his palms together like a crook about to cash in on a landslide. "That's it for you, then, March. Find a pretty woman and celebrate our success with a night on the town." He paused and waggled his bushy brows. "I know that's what I'm going to do."

A pretty woman. If only it were that simple.

Neil thanked the doctor and set off determinedly for his office. There was something he needed to do, something he'd been putting off. And it had nothing to do with celebrating.

He had nothing to celebrate.

"Jason," he announced to his startled secretary as he strode off the elevator into his penthouse office. "Get on the phone with Pattie in PR and tell her to meet me in my office in ten minutes. You come, too."

Jason nodded, politely averting his gaze to the files in his arms.

But his slack jaw was reminiscent of gawking, however courteous his eyes were being, and Neil tensed. "It's okay, Jas. You can look."

Jason mumbled an apology and jabbed his index finger several times at the elevator's down button.

Neil sighed and took a seat behind his desk. He'd better get used to that kind of reaction. Those who didn't know him would no doubt wonder at his scars; those who did, those who knew the whole story—or at least what he'd made known of it—thought the subject was too touchy to bring up in his presence.

For a brief moment he wished he had someone to talk to, someone to unload on. But opening up his feelings to another person wasn't an option. It was a completely foreign notion to the heart of this hardened businessman.

Once, he thought with a wisp of nostalgia, he had that kind of relationship with God. There was a time when his every care went straight to the Father's willing ears—but not now.

Now he felt God must turn a deaf ear to his cries. It was impossible to consider that God might forgive him for Peter Carlton's death. Just as Maddie was unable to forgive.

Neil shook his head to clear his thoughts. Now was not the time to be dwelling on his inner torment. He had business to attend to.

With a discreet knock, Jason and Pattie entered the room, each carrying a steno pad and a pen.

Neil stood and gestured them to chairs. "Have a seat. We've got a lot of ground to cover this afternoon."

The two practically scrambled into their chairs, making Neil feel like an ogre. He'd always treated his coworkers with respect, though recently he'd become distant and broody.

But he knew instinctively that it wouldn't help to apologize, so he cut to the chase. He gave Pattie a direct look, and when she returned it with the quiet confidence born from years of working under him, he asked, "What have you got lined up for the Parade of Lights?"

"Meaning?" she asked, wriggling her pen between her fingers.

"Have you finished planning the float? What's the theme? Have you begun preparations?"

"Everything's done," Pattie said, efficiently brushing a speck of lint from the hem of her green velvet skirt. "Down to the last twinkling light."

Neil swung his chair away from them, staring unseeing at the high-rise across the way. His stomach was in knots. In the back of his mind, he'd hoped nothing had been done yet. But it was really no surprise. The Parade of Lights was an annual event for March's. He had anticipated problems. He'd just hoped beyond hope to avoid them. He blew out a breath and continued. "And the theme is…?"

"In keeping with the Christmas season," Jason piped up. "You know, Santa and the elves. We've even got a pair of real reindeer. That ought to be a hit."

Neil swiveled back to face his colleagues

and steepled his fingers thoughtfully. "Isn't there a Santa Claus finale in this parade?"

"Well," stammered Jason, "yes. But—"

"And aren't we going to confuse the kiddies by presenting more than one Santa?"

Even Pattie's face blanched at Neil's grim statement. She hazarded a worried glance at Jason, who frowned back.

"We've clearly made an error in judgment here," Jason began hesitantly. "But I don't think we can change anything this late in the game."

"I do." Neil stood and paced the carpet, combing his fingers through the curls at the back of his neck. "You've got lots of glitter and snow, right?"

"Yes," came Pattie's prompt reply.

"Great." Neil felt the smallest tremor of enthusiasm pierce his quavering insides. He wondered if the others noticed how his voice lightened. "Then it's simple, really."

Pattie and Jason waited silently, their pens poised.

Neil's mind flashed briefly to Maddie. When he revealed himself, he wanted at least a small element of fantasy to cushion the blow. "This parade is for the kids, right?"

Jason nodded and gripped the corners of his steno pad. Pattie tapped her pen against her teeth.

"And what was the top children's movie of the season?"

"The remake of Cinderella," the two chorused.

"And the top-selling toy this Christmas?"

"The talking Cinderella doll!" Pattie announced, bounding from the chair in her excitement.

"Yes!" Neil exclaimed. He was having *fun* planning a parade for children. The thought surprised and amazed him. All this time he had had the opportunity to do something for others, and he'd been too lost in his own dull business world, brooding over his secret pain.

Though if he were honest, his plans were as much for Maddie and Nicky as they were for the other children. His pulse increased with the thought of the pleasure he might bring them. At first, anyway.

Pattie's eyes began to glitter. "I see this!" She nodded slowly, holding up her hands as if framing a picture. "We've got the fluffy clouds and glitter—"

"Right," Neil cut in, warming to his spur-of-the-moment solution. "We add lots of gold and silver. Can we get plenty of flashing lights?"

"Done," said Jason, slapping a palm on his notebook with a crack that reverberated through the office.

"And Cinderella?" Neil queried.

"I'll contact the costumer immediately." Pattie scribbled furiously in her notebook. "Nix the elves. Enter Cinderella."

"There's a real nice gal who works the cosmetic counter. Maybe she could... That is..." Jason's sentence trailed off as he adjusted his tie.

Neil was amused by the flush that rose on the young man's cheeks. He cocked an eyebrow and grinned. "She could...?" he prompted.

"Er...make a pretty Cinderella?" Jason finished in a rush of breath.

"Sign her up," said Neil decisively, regaining his seat behind the desk. "Pattie?"

"Sir?"

"I can trust you to all the details, yes?"

"Of course." She and Jason moved to exit the office.

"Oh, and Pattie..." Neil called as if remembering a last-minute thought.

"Yes?"

"Be sure and order a costume for Prince Charming while you're at it."

"Prince Charming?" Jason repeated, looking vaguely alarmed.

Neil chuckled. "Of course. Can't have Cinderella without Prince Charming."

"And…who would that be?" Pattie asked tentatively.

Neil winked and smiled broadly. "I already have someone in mind."

Chapter Eight

Rory.

Even the thought of his name sent warm fuzzies skittering around her heart and paradoxical shivers of delight trailing down her spine. Maddie couldn't wait to be with him again, to inhale the scent of his spicy cologne, to gaze into his velvety dark eyes.

But how was she ever going to find him? How would he ever find her?

The crowds, lured by an unusually warm winter's evening, had come out in droves for the first night of the Parade of Lights. Elbowing and jostling one another for the best spots to view the spectacle, they swarmed the sidewalks and street corners.

Chances of finding Rory in this mess were slim to none. She strained to recognize his dark head of hair and broad shoulders, searched face after face for her bandaged Phantom—but with no success.

She and Nicky had only covered one city block. The parade route was over a mile. Compounding the problem was the fact that the parade went on for a full seven days.

Meet me at the Parade of Lights.

She ground her teeth in frustration. Why hadn't he told her something more specific? Where? When?

What if she never saw him again?

"Mom? Is it starting yet?" Nicky pulled at her sleeve and gestured to the street, his eyes glowing in childish delight.

It wasn't a cold night, but she'd bundled Nicky and herself in their long johns and goose-down parkas anyway, certain that as the night deepened they'd need them. Right now, though, she was feeling sticky and hot.

And frustrated.

If she *did* find Rory, the first order of business would be getting his last name and a phone number. After she strangled him for putting her through this, that is. Would it have been that difficult for him to name a specific night? A street corner? This was utter madness. She didn't need the extra stress.

What she *did* need was to find out once and for all who Rory was, and why he was being so mysterious about his identity. Again, she scanned the crowds for his tall, broad form and bandaged face.

Where is he? her mind screamed. What if he wasn't here? What if she'd come on the wrong night? If she had to, she thought, clenching her fists, she'd come back every night for a week.

Not that it would make any difference. She would never find Rory in this sea of faces.

A marching band proclaimed the start of the parade and Nicky dragged her to the street corner. "Look, Mom!" A fluorescent blue-and-gold banner held by four young band members announced that the event was sponsored by March's Department Store.

Maddie's stomach turned queasy. Even the slightest reminder of that man could still set her off, and she fought against the angry tears that threatened in the corners of her eyes.

Why was it that she couldn't even read the name of the department store without breaking down? She'd always considered herself stronger than that.

She *was* stronger than that. She bit the inside of her lip. She had to get over it. So what if Neil March sponsored the event? She was here to find Rory.

Or rather, for him to find her. He'd *promised*. And somehow, despite the rational side of her brain telling her that it could never happen, she believed him.

She settled back on the edge of the sidewalk, pulling Nicky over her crossed legs, wrapping her arms tightly around him and giving him a sound kiss on the cheek.

"Mom!" he protested, squirming at the personal affront to his dignity.

She chuckled as he wiggled away from her with a scowl. "Look, Nick. Clowns!"

The boy was instantly entranced, forgetting all about his mother's outrageous and offensive public display of affection. Maddie sighed and wrapped her arms around her knees. She might as well enjoy the parade, though she might be seeing a lot of it in the next week.

A clown riding a stuffed camel that he manipulated with his hands approached her, nuzzling the camel's nose into her neck.

Maddie searched the man's eyes, but they

were a pale blue, not the obsidian-black eyes she sought.

She was getting desperate, looking for Rory's face even in a painted clown's. She laughed at herself and slapped the stuffed animal away. The clown shrugged and moved on, allowing Nicky to pat the camel's head.

She didn't know how Rory might be disguised, or even *if* he'd be disguised, much less *in* the parade. But if he were, he wouldn't be a clown.

Her mind flashed to the sexy, dark Phantom of the Opera she'd first met. The image fit him splendidly. The tall, broad-shouldered man with smoldering dark eyes. A mystery man who moved silently and unexpectedly into her life, sweeping her into a romantic fairy tale and then disappearing once again into the darkness of the night.

I'll find you. She smiled at the echo of the words, his rich baritone laughter haunting the corridors of her mind.

She pulled her thoughts back to the present as a large, glittering float arrived, flashing with hundreds of tiny colored lights. Gaily wrapped presents topped the float, along with several friendly elves, waving, smiling and tossing handfuls of candy to eager children.

Her eyes shifted to Nicky, and her hand snaked out to grab the back of his parka. The boy knew better than to run into the street, but other children were diving for candy, and she was afraid that in his excitement Nicky would forget the rules.

The float passed, followed by a marching band. Another glittery float was on its way. Taking a deep breath, Maddie stretched back on her hands and closed her eyes.

A shower of cellophane-wrapped candy landed directly in her lap. Startled, she looked up onto the float, into the familiar, haunting dark eyes of her Phantom.

His smile faded when she stiffened, reading the banner that proclaimed the float to be compliments of March's Department Store. What was he doing on *that* float?

She realized with a start that his face was no longer bandaged or masked. And he was costumed as Prince Charming, his thick shoulders covered with a familiar black cape, though the rest of the outfit was new.

Why was he on March's float? She'd known he was a wealthy businessman. An upper-level executive. Everything about him reeked power and affluence.

Her mind fled from the obvious answer, the answer she read in his dark, expressive eyes. Eyes that burned with pain. And truth.

He wasn't hiding from cameras and reporters now. He wasn't trying to hide from her probing gaze, either. He was on center stage, and she knew instinctively that he meant himself to be there, and for Maddie to see him.

Prince Charming. Was it a fluke, or a message?

It was clear that the others on the float deferred to him, though he was beaming his customary kind smile at everyone. It was equally clear she'd made a terrible mistake.

He couldn't be Neil March. He just *couldn't*. He had said his name was Rory.

But he hadn't admitted his last name.

He's March's CEO, she thought. *And he was too embarrassed to tell me.* Her mind screamed for a logical explanation. Anything but the truth. Anything that would make her nightmare go away, make the knot in the pit of her stomach loosen, make her throat stop constricting before it strangled her.

Neil March.

Her Phantom, the kind, gentle man who had been romancing her was Neil March.

The spiked realization hit her with all the fury of an ice storm, and she wondered for an agonizing moment if she were going to be sick, right here in front of all these people.

She glared at him, daring him to deny the silent accusation in her eyes.

His jaw tightened and he nodded, his eyes pleading with her to understand. The glow from the lights on the float wasn't enough for her to distinguish the features he'd hidden— first with the mask, and then with the bandage. But even in the shadows, he was strikingly handsome, his beautiful, compelling dark eyes even now luring her, causing her heart to soften under his gaze.

She turned away, wrapping her arms tightly around her rib cage. Willing herself not to fall apart. Not now. Not in front of him.

She forced herself to take slow, even breaths, though her lungs were screaming for more oxygen and she felt dizzy with confusion.

Neil March. How could it be?

Neil waited, willing her to turn back, his soul begging hers to understand. He'd taken a huge risk tonight, going public—not only with her, but with the world—for the first time since his accident.

If only she would turn back. That first look, when shock had given way to recognition, had nearly toppled him from the float, so intense, so angry was the glare. Hatred sparked from her eyes, as he had known it would—though he had prayed desperately that it wouldn't.

But that was nothing compared to the emptiness he felt when she turned away. His chest was so hollow he wasn't even certain his heart continued to beat.

Why wouldn't she turn around, confront him with her anger? He was ready to hop down from the float right now, face whatever he had coming to him.

He shouldn't have come tonight. He should have figured out some way to tell her, to explain. He was an idiot, displaying himself on March's float. He'd taken a risk and it had backfired on him.

She'd never understand. And how could he explain?

He clamped his jaw until his teeth hurt. His beautiful, fiery Maddie. He expected her to fight, to yell, to pummel his chest with her fists. But not this. Never this. Why had she turned away?

Neil thrust both hands into the bucket of candy and tossed them blindly to the clamoring children. He couldn't make out faces anymore. His vision had blurred.

He swiped a hand down his face, willing himself to face the crowds, the reporters, the questions.

Eventually, he would have to find Maddie. And *try* to undo the damage that his hollow chest told him was beyond repair. If only he could.

He glanced behind him, hoping beyond hope that his gaze would meet hers, that she would beckon to him. But she was looking in the other direction, staring fiercely through a marching band.

His arms felt suddenly heavy, so heavy he could barely lift the candy from the bucket. He couldn't do this anymore: play the happy, benevolent executive. The thought made him sick to his stomach.

He'd had enough pretending—for one lifetime and then some. With a tired sigh, he jumped from the float and disappeared into the darkness.

* * *

Maddie refused to turn back until she was certain the March float was long gone. Nicky was exclaiming over the little cars driven by fez-topped men.

"Nicky, let's go," she ground out from between clenched teeth, but her son didn't hear. He crowed in delight over another marching band, pointing and laughing at the crashing cymbals.

Maddie tightened her fists. She'd just have to wait it out.

She shivered in apprehension. What if Rory... if *Neil* came to see her? How could she face him after...

He had *kissed* her, she recalled suddenly. Even after he knew who she was. They'd become close, emotionally tied to each other. At least she'd thought they had. She had very nearly given her heart to this man. Her foolish heart.

Scrubbing her lips with the sleeve of her coat, she cursed the man who had given life back to her, only to rip it cruelly from her again.

She felt violated. Polluted by a man with a heart of ice.

He didn't know who you were the night you met, her fickle mind whispered. Maddie swallowed hard.

No wonder he'd run away when he found out who she was. He'd been just as shocked as she to discover the paradox of their relationship.

Or had he? Was this all some kind of game to him? Had he known who she was from the beginning? Had he been using her for his own amusement?

Her mind flashed back to the ball, to the way her Phantom had picked her from the crowd as if he'd been waiting just for her. Had he known? Was he laughing at her vulnerability, making sport of her?

But *Rory,* her Rory. He was so kind, so gentle. She could see it in his dark eyes. He put others' needs before his own. The concern in his eyes when Nicky was lost—could any man feign that?

He had shown her how to laugh again.

He *cared* for her. And for Nicky.

But Rory was Neil. Neil was Rory. Her mind seesawed, trying to make the two balance. But it was impossible—completely irreconcilable.

"Maddie." The low, rich baritone whispered on the wind behind her.

She whirled, wondering if her mind was playing tricks on her.

He looked regal, if chilly, in sparkling gold tights and a snow-white tunic. Rory was every inch Prince Charming, from the top of his crowned head to the toes of his soft leather, knee-high boots.

It was a crime for a man to be so blatantly handsome, Maddie thought uncharitably. Especially when that man was Neil March. She looked away, trying to gather her unruly thoughts together again.

Dragging in a breath for courage, she scanned his face, which was now free of any bandages. *She* wasn't the one who should be squirming here. If he had come looking for a fight, he was going to get one—and good! She wasn't about to back down. *She* was the offended party, and he wasn't going to intimidate her with his good looks and charm.

Her eyes met his and held. If it were possible, his eyes were even more piercing unmasked and unbandaged, though the skin around his right eye was lighter than the rest of his face, and a scar arched over his right temple.

On another man, the scar would have marred his perfection, but if anything, it enhanced Rory's features. *Neil's* features.

"You know who I am," he rasped, sounding as if his breath was being cut off.

Maddie nodded, fighting to control the anger that surged in furious waves into her head and extremities until she thought she might burst from rage. It was cold. *So cold.* Cascades of anger felt like warm water on frostbitten fingers. It hurt, terribly, but the alternative was so much worse. She embraced her anger, nurturing it, allowing it to warm her.

"How could you?" she exclaimed, crossing her arms in front of her to keep from pounding his chest. "What kind of game are you playing, Rory? Or Neil? Or whatever your name is?"

He stood silently, his jaw clenched.

"What? You can't even answer me now? You had all the answers before. Knew just what to do, just what to say to make poor, stupid Maddie Carlton buy the whole act. You must be laughing now."

His dark eyes clouded and he shook his head. "Maddie, I'm—"

"You're a liar. And a cheat, you piece of

trash. And if I ever lay eyes on you again it will be too soon."

Nicky turned around, evidently distracted by his mother's harsh tone. He stood in surprise when he saw Neil, who hunkered down to the boy's size. "Mommy, it's the Fireman!" he exclaimed, rushing into Neil's outstretched arm.

"No, honey," Maddie ground out. "Mr. March isn't a fireman. This is Rory, the man we saw at the zoo the other day."

Neil ruffled the boy's parka hood and stood, smiling briefly when the boy patted his leg affectionately.

Maddie, her blood still pulsing in her veins, mentally coaxed herself to calm down. She was an adult, after all, and Neil March couldn't hurt her any more than he already had. She had nothing in her chest but a resounding emptiness. He had taken her heart and trampled it into the dust. She had nothing more to fear from him.

He stood silently, his hands hanging loosely at his sides. She could see the tension in his neck and jaw, but his eyes had cleared.

"Let me explain—" he said finally, his voice low and even.

"You've got nothing to say that I want to hear. Just get away from me."

He stepped forward and grasped her elbow, holding fast when she tried to pull away from his grasp. "Not until you hear what I have to say."

Maddie fought with the urge to clamp her hands over her ears and scream, "La, la, la, la, la!" the way she had when she was a child and didn't want to hear what was being said. Instead she just glared at him.

He raised a dark eyebrow.

"Be my guest, Rory. *Neil*," she corrected sarcastically.

"You don't have to call me Neil," he said quietly. "I went by Rory as a child. Neil Rory March III. Already had a Senior and Junior, so I was relegated to my middle name."

She didn't want to call him his pet name from childhood. She didn't want to call him anything. She just wanted to run away. But he still had a tight grip on the sleeve of her parka and was planted firmly, legs braced, on the street corner.

She could scream, make a scene, but she dropped that notion the moment it entered her head. She was in the public light too much as it was. The best idea was to give him the silent treatment—a regular dose of his own medicine. She lifted her chin and looked away.

"I never meant to hurt you."

"No? Funny, that's not the way I see it." So much for her silent treatment. Rory had a way of nudging her out of her shell even when she was belligerently refusing to cooperate. "I think you had all this planned from the beginning. I think you set me up. I think you're the lowest slimeball ever to call himself a human being."

He laughed dryly. "You can't call me anything I haven't already called myself."

Pain veiled his expression, and for one brief moment, Maddie felt her heart capitulating. She almost felt sorry for him. Almost believed his pleading, flaming eyes. They were Rory's eyes. Gentle, loving eyes. Eyes a woman could lose herself in. *Almost*.

"Okay, so supposing—and I find it hard to believe—but just supposing you are telling the truth. You didn't know who I was when you waltzed in the door of the ballroom. That you picked me out of the crowd was just some strange coincidence." She paused and hammered her finger into his chest. "You still could have told me the truth. When I took off my mask, you *knew*. And you didn't say a word."

He nodded. "I knew." He brushed his fingers over the back of her hand—a tender, intimate caress. "And I should have faced up to you then. I should have revealed the truth behind my mask."

He forced himself to meet her angry gaze, dragging a deep breath of air to will courage into his lungs. The crisp air stung and he took another gulp. Any feeling, even pain, was better than emptiness. "But, Maddie, I couldn't help myself. That night was like magic for me. It was the first time since…"

He paused and cleared his throat. "I don't go out in public much. Then I saw you, looking so small and alone, so lovely and clearly out of your element. I just had to rescue you. And when we danced, and talked, it opened up a part of me that I didn't even know still existed. You made me laugh again, think about the future without cringing. I never wanted that moment to end. I never wanted *us* to end."

"Harrumph." Her bitter laugh sounded almost like a snort.

"That's right. Once I knew who you were, I

knew it could never happen. I ran away, pure and simple."

"No, you didn't," Maddie said, her voice a low monotone and her gaze piercing him with accusation. "Are you going to tell me you didn't know I'd be there at the grand opening of the Pachyderm Pavilion? That you hadn't come specifically to see me? Are you going to lie again, Rory?"

"No. You don't understand." He thrust both hands through his hair. She wasn't listening. She'd worked it all out in her head, thought she knew all the answers.

But she didn't. She couldn't.

How could he tell her...?

"No? Astonish me." Her tone was acerbic, colder than the ice forming on the streets.

"I wish I could," he bit back. "What do you want me to say, Maddie? That I went to the zoo looking for you? Okay, I did. But I didn't plan for you to see me. I didn't plan—" His sentence dropped into silence. *To kiss you. To fall in love with you.*

Her cheeks were flaming. Even angry, she was the most beautiful, desirable woman Neil had ever known. He stamped down the urge to kiss the pretty pout off her lips. It would only make matters worse. Even more to the point, he had no right.

"You manipulated me! You—you made me talk about—"

"About me. Yes. But not for the reason you think. I was trying to figure out how to tell you." He stopped and glanced at a passing float, but it blurred before his eyes. "I know you hate me, Maddie. I know I should have revealed my identity that first night we met. But I didn't. And then I couldn't. And then…"

He paused and reached for her, caressing the satiny skin of her cheek with his thumb.

She didn't pull away, though he could feel the tension pulsing through her muscles. "And then," he repeated, "I didn't want to. I wanted to be anyone in the world but Neil March. I wanted to be…your Rory."

Maddie stood transfixed. His touch was so light, so gentle, yet it sent waves of electricity into her heart. These weren't the enemy's hands cupping her cheek, stroking her hair. They were Rory's hands. It was Rory's face drawing near, Rory's mouth covering her own.

"Rory," she whispered as her arms slipped around his waist.

"Maddie." His voice was tortured.

She stiffened as if hit by a bolt of lightning. It wasn't Rory kissing her. It was *Neil March*. They were one and the same. How could she have forgotten, even for a moment? This was the man responsible for Peter's death.

With a strangled sob, she pushed him away. "Get away from me," she rasped through a closed throat. "Just get away from me. I don't ever want to see you again." She turned away from him, focusing on the parade.

"If you'd just give me a chance to make it up to you. To prove myself."

His breath was warm on her neck, but she would not, *could not* respond. Suddenly the cacophony of voices around them swelled. She glanced around, aware that more than one spectator was caught up in *their* spectacle instead of the parade.

She was making a scene. And it was his fault. "Go away," she snapped.

"Okay." His voice was more than resigned, it was devoid of feeling. But the flame in his eyes when he turned her around by the shoulders was anything but empty. "But I want you to know something before I go."

She gasped for air. Though his hands were on her shoulders, she felt that she was strangling. She tried to speak—to scream her hatred, her contempt—but nothing came from her dry throat but a small whimper of protest.

"You are the most magnificent woman I've ever met, Maddie Carlton. You have so much to live for. Grab on to life and experience it for all it's worth." His voice was low. "You deserve it."

His gaze probed hers for a moment longer, then he swiveled away from her and strode into the shadows. She stood silently and watched him go. Not knowing what to feel. Not wanting to feel at all.

"And, Maddie?"

His rich baritone came from the darkness. She didn't answer, but waited—her fingernails biting into the soft flesh of her palm—for his final words.

"That wasn't blood money I sent you. Not some form of penance. I know there's no salvation for me. I haven't shied away from my responsibilities. I wear them around my neck like a noose."

She heard his footsteps as he strode away. It was over, and a part of her was glad.

But another, deeper part of her grieved. Grieved for what was…for what might have been.

Why couldn't Neil March have been the savage beast she had imagined him to be? Why did he have to be so…human?

And why did she care?

Chapter Nine

"*Do you want to tell me what's going on?*"

"*Hmm?*" *Peter replied absently, looking through a rack of ties.*

Maddie felt her pulse pounding against her temples, drowning out the sound of bustling Christmas shoppers looking for last-minute gifts.

Why was he playing dumb? Did he think she was a fool?

He must. He'd been staying out late, sneaking around. And once...once a woman had phoned and promptly hung up when she discovered Peter wasn't available.

She swallowed, grimacing as her throat tightened. Her stomach churned. She could still remember the tinkle of the woman's laugh, and it grated like salt in a wound.

Her blood pressure rose a notch as she observed Peter moving nonchalantly from aisle to aisle as if he hadn't a care in the world. Out on a jaunt with his wife and his son, and happy to be there.

Except that it was a lie.

Maddie couldn't put her finger on it, but something in their relationship had changed.

Tiny drops of perspiration beaded on her forehead. "You're hiding something, Peter," she said, latching on to the sleeve of his jacket. "And don't you even try to deny it."

Peter stopped walking and whirled to confront her, his face grim. His eyes, usually so warm and friendly, turned to crystal-blue ice, entirely erasing the congenial laugh lines that ordinarily spoke volumes about his personality.

The mall blurred around her until all she could focus on was Peter's angry face. She squeezed her son's hand, a last-ditch effort to cling to her sanity. She was drifting off the edge, and had no idea how far she would fall.

"Don't go there, Maddie," he said, his voice low and severe. "Just don't. It won't do anyone any good."

Maddie barely restrained herself from pum-

meling his chest. She wanted to claw his heart out with her hands, because that's exactly what she felt he was doing with his cold, callous words.

She dropped Nicky's hand and squeezed her fists tightly until she could feel her fingernails biting into her palms. The pain was reassuring in a world that was going topsy-turvy.

He hadn't even bothered to deny her unspoken accusation.

"So I'm just supposed to smile and drop it?" she asked in her most cutting tone.

Peter actually smiled, his laugh lines reappearing as if by magic. He beseeched her with his gigantic blue eyes—the little-boy look he used to get his way with her. "I wish you would."

Maddie's mouth dropped open in astonishment. She'd practically accused him of cheating on her, of betraying their sacred vows, and he had the gall to smile at her as if there was nothing amiss between them.

"I don't think so," Maddie exclaimed, causing Nicky to cling to her leg. She reached down and patted his back, wishing she could be likewise comforted.

If only Peter would deny everything, take

*her in his arms and reassure her of his love...
but he'd turned his attention to a display of
leather wallets.*

*"I think," Maddie said through clenched
teeth, "that we'll talk about it* now.*"*

*"Maddie, we're in the middle of a mall,"
Peter said calmly. "Now is not the time." He
paused and rubbed his jaw. "But I can see that
I've upset you. Perhaps I've made an error in
judgment. I guess I'd better 'fess up—but I'm
not going to do it in a mall."*

*An error in judgment? Choosing the wrong
restaurant was an error in judgment. What
Peter had done—what he'd practically admitted out loud—went far beyond an error in
judgment. He had betrayed the woman he had
promised in front of God and witnesses to love,
honor and cherish.*

Till death do us part.

Maddie rolled over, clutching her pillow.

*"You call what you've done to me an error
in judgment?" Maddie exclaimed, unable even
now to voice the words.*

Cheating. Adultery.

Her pulse pounded in her head. Only be-

latedly did she realize that she had shouted, when several nearby shoppers stopped to gape openmouthed at her, then turn expectantly toward the object of her wrath.

"What I've done to you?" Peter repeated softly. His eyes met hers, and then his face blanched to a deathly white as understanding dawned on him.

Anger crossed his face, then disappointment. "Nicky, come here," Peter said in a low, firm voice, which the little boy immediately interpreted and obeyed.

Nicky willingly detached himself from his mother's leg and, with a yelp of excitement, threw himself into his father's waiting arms.

"We," he said to Nicky, but met Maddie's eyes over their son's head, "are going to visit Santa's Workshop."

The message in his eyes was clear. She was not invited.

"What do you say to that, champ?" he asked when Nicky began wriggling in his arms. "Want to go visit the elves?"

He set the boy on the floor and laughingly followed as Nicky pulled him toward the sparkling exhibit.

He didn't look back.

"Guess I'll be shopping," Maddie said to herself as her two boys, as she'd once affectionately thought of them, disappeared into the snow-white cotton drifts that marked the entrance to the workshop.

She'd no sooner turned her back on the display than she heard a deafening whoosh. *Moments later she was nearly knocked from her feet by a scorching heat.*

Terror closed in around her. Her stomach knotted. She stopped breathing.

"No," she moaned, startling herself into half wakefulness. She punched her pillow and curled back into a ball, her eyes fluttering shut as sleep once again washed over her.

In what felt like slow motion, she turned to see what she already pictured in her mind.

She could hear someone screaming as if from a distance.

It was her own voice.

"Nicky! Peter!"

The entrance to the workshop was a wall of flame. The cotton clouds of snow and glitter welcomed the blaze.

She stood transfixed, her heart and her mind numb. This couldn't be happening.

It couldn't be.

It seemed like torturous hours, but it must have been only moments later when someone knocked into her from behind, nearly sending her sprawling.

Stripping his shirt from his back, the man didn't stop to apologize, but dived into the flame-encased workshop. His shirt, placed haphazardly over his nose and mouth, seemed meager protection from the smoke, but it was clear the man was bent on being a hero.

That brief contact, when the man knocked into her, was all Maddie needed to be spurred into action. Following the man's lead, she dashed toward the flames, not bothering to find any measure of protection for herself. She was thinking with her heart, and her heart said that her beloved husband and little boy were in there.

How she would rescue them she didn't know. She only knew that she must try.

Just as she was poised to throw herself into the flames, someone dived for her heels and sent her tumbling. She was quickly and un-graciously pulled away by her feet, but not without protest. She fought and wriggled and scratched, but the old woman she battled with had a bruising grip on her ankles.

Maddie knew she was screaming and crying, but she didn't care. Tears blurred her vision.

"You don't understand," she begged her well-intentioned assailant. "My son! My husband! They are in that inferno! Oh, God help them, please," she prayed aloud.

The woman helped Maddie prop herself against a wall, leaving a firm hand on Maddie's shoulder—whether to comfort or restrain her Maddie couldn't tell.

"They are doing all they can," she said before Maddie could protest further. "The firemen just arrived," the woman continued. "It's going to be okay."

Maddie tried to speak, tried to ask about her husband and son, but nothing came out of her mouth except a pathetic whimper.

The woman looked at Maddie, and in her faded gray eyes Maddie could see the warmth of love, the pain of loss and the years of struggle.

And the light of hope and faith.

Maddie clung to that light as she clung to

the woman's gnarled hand. Her faith in God had seen her through difficulties before. Life was wrought with storms. She would simply ride this one out.

Maddie closed her eyes.

When she opened them, the woman was gone.

Maddie leaped to her feet and searched frantically through the thick crowd that had gathered. She knew in her heart the next hours could hold countless agony. She could not do it alone.

Somehow she had believed the woman would be there for her, to hold her hand through the ordeal.

But she was nothing more than a kind stranger. She probably had her own family to get home to.

What had the woman said? It's going to be okay. But how?

Maddie sucked in a deep breath and searched inside of herself for that still, small voice that reassured her that she was not alone. Shoulders set and jaw clenched in grim determination, she turned toward the burning display.

People swirled around her, jostled into her

in their rush to evacuate the building. The smoke alarm was blaring its shrill warning. Maddie ignored the people, ignored the warning to escape. She had to reach her son, her husband. No matter what.

A shirtless, soot-covered man stumbled from the inferno, a small, drooping form in his arms.

"Nicky!" Maddie choked out the name.

Paramedics swept the boy from the man's arms just as Maddie rushed forward.

Oh, God, no! Her soul cried out to heaven as she approached the still, charcoal-dusted form of her son.

They were wrapping him in sterile bandages, gently coaxing an oxygen mask over his nose and mouth.

"Is he...?" Maddie stammered, touching the shoulder of a waiting paramedic. "I'm his mother."

"He's alive," the man said crisply.

Maddie's shoulders slumped in relief.

"But we're taking him to Children's Hospital. You can ride with him if you like." The man turned a grave face toward her. "He's hurt pretty badly, ma'am."

Maddie's breath caught in her throat. "Will he...?" she began again.

The paramedic's eyes clouded with compassion as he shook his head. "You'll have to wait until we get to the hospital."

"Of course," Maddie agreed dully, her voice nothing more than a squeak.

But what about Peter? He was still inside the blaze. How could she go with Nicky when Peter had yet to be rescued?

Her mind pulled for an answer while her heart pumped furiously.

Just as suddenly, she was enveloped with calm, and she reached for it, embraced it. She knew what to do.

Peter would want her to go with their son.

She turned toward the ambulance.

"Let me go!" The man's voice was low and threatening.

The sudden commotion momentarily distracted Maddie. She glanced over to see the soot-covered man who had rescued her son struggling between two uniformed firemen, who were holding him by his arms.

"Let me go!" the man demanded again, his voice coarse from smoke. He wrenched this way and that, clearly trying to dislodge himself from their grasp.

All Maddie could make out of the man was

his broad shoulders and coal-black hair. Or was that soot?

But when he turned his face toward her, she gasped in shock. One whole side of his face had been burned.

"I've got to go back in there!" the man insisted, seemingly unaware of his injury.

"You've been burned," one of the firemen reasoned, keeping his voice at a low, even timbre. "We're taking you to the hospital."

"No!" the man yelled, loud enough—despite the crowd—for the sound to echo off the walls. "I must go back! There's still a man in there!"

The firemen continued to restrain him.

As the ceiling of the workshop collapsed, there was a rushing sound and a billow of flame.

"No-o-o-o!" the soot-covered rescuer screamed, echoing the agony of her own heart.

"Peter!" Maddie cried simultaneously, reaching her arms out in a powerless gesture.

"P-e-e-e-t-e-r-r-r!"

Maddie sat bolt upright in bed, her spine ramrod straight and her hands clenched around sweat-soaked temples. Her feet thrashed around the blankets encasing her legs like a mummy.

It was only a dream. For a moment, her body sagged in relief.

That dream again.

Her muscles tightened as her mind wakened. The horrible nightmare was all too real. She hadn't dreamed the flames, the screaming. If only she really could wake up and make it all disappear.

She huddled into the twisted mound of bed-covers, rubbing her arms against the chill and fear-induced quivering. Coaching herself to take slow, even breaths, she offered a silent prayer that she hadn't wakened Nicky.

It wouldn't be the first time the small boy had stumbled sleepy-eyed into Mommy's bed-room to find out why she had screamed. She usually allowed him to crawl into bed with her, a soft, sweet warmth against the cold depths of her heart. She enjoyed tucking his sweet, downy head into her chest, hearing the smooth incantation of his breathing—a prayer with-out words.

But tonight she couldn't be strong for him, couldn't comfort him.

For once, *she* wanted to be the child.

No. Not a child, exactly. She wanted a man's thick, strong arms to wrap around her, protecting her from the world's angry darts. She wanted a firm chest to rest against, a broad shoulder to cry on.

She wanted Rory.

The memory of his dark, compassion-filled eyes flooded her mind, bringing with it a bittersweet combination of tension and relief.

Funny how her heart refused to acknowledge the truth about that man. He was, and always would be, Rory to her, however strongly her mind protested that the flame-eyed Phantom was none other than the despicable Neil March.

She couldn't—wouldn't—analyze the warmth that the mere thought of Rory brought to her insides, the way the memory of his voice soothed her churning emotions. To think of Rory was to tread on dangerous ground.

Squeezing her eyes shut, she curled tightly into a ball, her forehead tucked into her knees. A single sob escaped her throat, and she clenched her teeth against the avalanche of emotion threatening to consume her.

Nights were always the worst.

Why did God allow this to happen? To have

lost Peter, and to struggle daily with the unanswered questions, was bad enough. But now to fall in love with the man responsible for her husband's death…

She hiccuped, gulping for air with the high squeak of hyperventilation. It was as if all the oxygen had been squeezed from the room. Her lungs felt ready to collapse from overexertion.

"Why?" she whispered into her pillow. "Why did You make this happen?"

Once the words were uttered, she could no longer hold back the storm in her chest. She began to sob, brokenly at first, then in huge, heartrending wails barely muffled by her down pillow.

For the first time since she had met Rory, she let herself cry—really *cry* for her loss.

For what might have been, and never could be.

For Peter. For Nicky.

For Rory.

And though she thought she ought to be struck down by lightning for lashing out at God, she felt as though He had given her permission to vent, given her the opening she needed to grieve.

As her sobs wound down to an occasional

hiccup, she closed her eyes, relaxing into the pillow. Crying had forced her muscles to loosen, even those testy shoulder muscles that were ordinarily rock-hard expressions of her tension.

She drifted into half sleep, marveling at the wonder of a good cry. Bits of Scripture she'd learned as a child washed into her head, comforting her like a gentle hand stroking her sweat-soaked brow.

"'For My thoughts are not your thoughts, neither are your ways My ways,' declares the Lord."

"Trust in the Lord with all your heart, and lean not on your own understanding."

"He gathers the lambs in His arms and carries them close to His heart."

The darkness wrapped around Maddie like a home-made quilt.

Oh, to be a child again…. To know the security of a father watching over his beloved daughter. Maddie longed for safety. Ached for comfort.

With a tiny sigh, she squeezed her eyes shut and imagined a winged warrior in each corner of the bedroom, watching over her, guarding her against hurt and pain.

She could almost see her mother's face, young and fine-boned, whispering softly about how God sent his angels to watch over His children. Remembering the angels often helped her as a child; the thought of an angel in every corner was like a slew of night-lights piercing the darkness.

Even as a parent, it helped to remember the angels. Whenever she feared for Nicky's safety. Whenever life got beyond her control. They were there, watching over her, protecting her from the darkness of the night. She breathed a deep sigh of relief.

Maddie opened her eyes, half expecting the bright shimmer of angel swords around her bed. But of course there was nothing.

And yet...

As she had so often done as a child, Maddie fancied she drifted off to sleep to the soft whir of angel wings.

Chapter Ten

He was stalking her.

What else could you say about a man who lingered in the shadows, hoping to discover where she ate, where she shopped, where she went to relax and have a good time.

There might be prettier ways to describe it, but the truth was that Neil was following Maddie around almost as close as her own shadow.

Except that Maddie Carlton rarely left the house. Which left Neil standing on a cold street corner a good deal of the time.

The evening was crisp, and cold enough to turn his cowboy-boot-encased toes numb. He blew into his fingers, trying to restore circulation.

If he had the brains of an amoeba, he thought,

he'd forget about Maddie and go home where it was warm.

And empty.

Ever since he'd met Maddie, his house hadn't been the same. It hadn't been home. His servants couldn't give his house or his heart the warmth of love.

For that he needed Maddie. Someone to tend the fire in his hearth, bank the coals regularly. Someone to share with. Live with. Love with.

Maddie.

His heart jumped into his throat as he saw her slip out the front door, followed by an enthusiastic Nicky. His chest warmed at the sight of the boy. It was bad enough to be separated from Maddie, but he found himself wanting to spend time with Nicky, too.

He wanted them to be a family.

Stamping his feet against the cold, he watched as she drove her car out of the driveway. Then he pulled a helmet over his head, making sure the darkly shaded visor was firmly in place. He didn't want her to recognize him until he could approach her on his terms.

A moment later, he was on his motorcycle. Fortunately, the roads were free of ice, making his Harley a cold but convenient ride. At least on a motorcycle he could easily follow Maddie wherever she was going, weaving in and out of traffic, even taking shortcuts through back alleys if it became necessary. His lips closed in a straight, hard line. He was determined to speak to her.

To make her listen.

He'd considered putting his thoughts down in a letter and sending it to her, but rejected the idea, knowing she'd probably tear it to pieces without reading it once she realized it was from him.

If she could just get past her anger. She had felt something for him—Neil knew she had. At least she felt something for *Rory,* he thought with a grimace.

But he *was* Rory. He just had to make her understand that.

He paused, surprised, when she pulled into a dead-end street that ended at the local elementary school. Neil thought Nicky was old enough to attend school, though he wasn't certain. Was Maddie out for a parent-teacher conference or something? But Nicky was only in kindergarten. Did they even *have* parent-teacher conferences for kindergarteners?

He took a quick spin around the block to

give Maddie time to go inside the building. By the time he pulled into the parking lot, it was jam-packed with cars.

Clearly he was mistaken about her intentions, but it was to his advantage, he decided instantly. He could hide in the crowd and plan his strategy, wait to approach her when the time was right. It would be a good sight easier than barging in on a one-on-one meeting. Which he would have done, had circumstances been different. He *would* see Maddie tonight… if he had to buy a ladder and climb up to her balcony to do so.

He smiled. Romeo, he was not. He wasn't even sure which window was hers, though he could hazard an educated guess from his nights standing watch over her.

He chuckled at the thought, and found himself whistling as he entered the main doors to the school. Perhaps Nicky was in a performance of some sort. He wanted to be there for the boy—prove himself to both Nicky and Maddie.

Prove he would always be there.

He followed the noisy crowd into the gym and discovered some sort of carnival in progress. Booths were set up in a circular pattern along the outside, with a smaller circle in the middle facing out. Bright lights and fluorescent colors beckoned onlookers to try their luck, spend their money to benefit the school. Children were laughing, parents were talking. It was a family scene, and it warmed Neil's heart just to be there, however tenuous his current relationship might be.

This was what he wanted. To experience life with the uncorrupted joy of a child. To coach Little League. To come home to warm, happy nights in Maddie's arms.

He shoved his hands into the pockets of his jeans and began strolling from booth to booth. He kept one eye on the displays, and the other eye on the lookout for Maddie and her son.

As he stopped to purchase a bag of caramel corn from a vendor, he spotted them across the room. Nicky was leaning far into a booth, swinging a magnet-laden fishing pole into a pool of magnetic fish.

"Here," said Neil gruffly, handing the vendor a twenty-dollar bill. "Keep the change."

The man gawked at him openmouthed before recovering with a surprised, "Yes, sir!" The caramel corn was a fifty-cent treat.

Neil strode through the crowd, his eyes never

leaving Maddie's back. "For you," he said, thrusting the bag of popcorn into her hands.

Maddie looked startled.

Then angry.

"What are you—" she began, but Nicky turned around, having heard Neil's voice, and squealed excitedly.

"Hello, Mr. Fireman. Can you help me catch a fish?" the boy asked immediately. "Mommy can't fish."

Neil winked at Maddie, who continued to scowl. "Ah. I think she's exaggerating. I'll bet she's a natural." He plunked a dollar onto the counter and was promptly rewarded with a fishing pole, which he extended to Maddie.

"I'm *not* going to—" Maddie began again, but then appeared to back down at the sight of her son's fallen expression. "Oh, all right. But you can't say I didn't warn you!"

She stood with her arms crossed over her chest, holding the fishing pole at an awkward angle, while Neil leaned over Nicky, coaching him on the best way to catch a magnetic fish.

"Wait until you see his mouth beginning to open," he whispered in the boy's ear. "Keep your pole low and steady."

Nicky, his face scrunched in concentration, did just as Neil said.

"Good, good. Now, here it comes...easy... easy..."

"I got him!" Nicky crowed triumphantly, yanking on the pole to reveal a red plastic fish. "I really got him!"

"Of course you did, sport!" Neil said affectionately, slapping Nicky a high five. "I knew you'd be a great fisherman. Just like your mother," he concluded with a pointed look toward Maddie.

"Of all the—" she muttered, leaning against the counter of the display. With a harrumph, she slung her fishing pole over her shoulder. "I can't believe I let you talk me into this," she said, shaking her head at her son.

"And *you!*" Neil felt her glare pierce him. "There are no words to tell you how despicable, how—"

Neil glanced behind her and raised his eyebrows. Dangling from the fishing line she had inadvertently tossed into a pond was a fluorescent-pink magnetic fish.

"I'm going to wipe that grin off your face with my...popcorn," she finished lamely.

"Before you do that," Neil said with a wry grin, "you might want to remove that fish from your pole." He wiggled his index finger at the glaring pink fish.

Nicky clapped his hands in delight. "Way to go, Mom. You caught a fish!"

"I *what?*" Maddie exclaimed, glancing over her shoulder. "I...but I only..."

"I happen to know," said Neil in a conspiratorial stage whisper, laying a gentle arm across the boy's shoulder, "that your mother is an excellent fisherwoman!"

"You happen to know *nothing,*" she barked, grabbing for Nicky's wrist and yanking him to the next display.

Neil sighed. For a moment he'd thought things were going relatively well. Better than he had expected, even.

But now—again—she was turning hostile.

"Maddie, wait!" Neil called, waving his arm. "I need to talk to you." He strode to where she stood glaring at the display of balloons in the next booth.

"We have nothing to talk about," she snapped. "Why don't you just leave me alone!"

Neil took a step back, wounded by her words.

He felt a raging need to justify himself warring in his chest with the dampening reminder that he couldn't justify himself even if he wanted to. He was guilty. It was his fault that Maddie's husband had died.

Maybe Maddie was right. He should turn around, walk away and never return. Become a recluse on some deserted island. Or at the very least hole himself up in his office.

But he couldn't let it go, and the anger surging through his veins made him reckless. If he couldn't beg and plead his way into her life, maybe a shock tactic would work.

"You had more than a few words about Neil March when you thought I was Rory. Why can't you say them to my face?"

Her cheeks blanched, then shaded with anger. She opened her mouth as if to speak, then slammed it closed again and bulldozed past him without a word.

He hadn't really expected her to blow up at him. She was too kind for that. Whatever she thought about him privately, she wouldn't air their dirty laundry in public. He wasn't even sure that she would confront him if it were just the two of them.

And if he didn't get her to release her anger toward him, he could never make her love him.

It was crazy. Two years ago Neil had lived without a care, wallowing in the jet-set lifestyle that was his heritage. Marrying and starting a family had been the furthest thing from his mind.

And now here was a ready-made family: a family he had neither earned nor deserved, yet he wanted them more than he'd ever wanted anything in his life. He wanted his arms, his heart, his *life*, full of Maddie Carlton and her son.

His gaze followed her profile as she escorted Nicky to a booth on the opposite corner of the gym. The woman would drive him insane! He plowed his fingers through the curls at the back of his neck, massaging the tension from his muscles.

After a moment of indecision, he shrugged his coat over his shoulders. He wasn't accomplishing anything by standing around staring at her.

Except perhaps stirring the flames of his own misery.

He threaded his way through the crowd, in-tent on his exit. A shrill scream stopped him in his tracks.

The scream was immediately followed by a loud splash and a round of applause. The rescuer in Neil relaxed. He turned just in time to see a soaking wet, gray-haired old woman emerge laughing and huffing from a four-foot pool of water.

The sight of the old-fashioned dunking booth brought a smile to Neil's face as he recalled his own childhood. He remembered an especially fond incident when his sharp aim and strong arm had landed his junior-high principal in the water and Neil on the baseball team.

He'd bet his last dollar that the woman cheerfully climbing from the pool was the principal of the school. A chuckle emerged from his lips as he stepped forward, rummaging through his pockets for some small change.

Just for old times' sake, he'd nail this principal a good one.

He tossed the boy behind the counter a handful of change and hefted a softball, tossing it into the air with a grin. The red-and-black target was only about ten feet away and was at least the size of a paper plate. It would be an easy mark. The booth was really set up for kids around Nicky's age.

Suddenly an idea came to Neil with such unexpected clarity that he nearly dropped his softball. Instead, he slammed the shot into the bull's-eye, sending a flailing, wet principal down for another dunk in the pool.

He ignored the cheerful crowd and moved around to the back of the booth, knocking on the makeshift door he found there. A portly, balding man answered, his curiosity giving way to jovial laughter as Neil explained his intentions.

With half an eye, Maddie watched her son throwing darts at water balloons. Her mind was whirling in tormented circles.

Why was Rory here? What did he want?

There was only one logical answer to the first question: he had followed her here. As to *why* he had followed her, Maddie couldn't begin to guess. The man was as much a mystery to her now as when he had been wearing his Phantom's mask.

Try as she might, she could not make her impression of Rory into Neil March. It just couldn't be done. One of those men was an illusion, and Maddie was simply too gun-shy to make the discovery on her own. If she risked her heart and bet on Rory, and it turned out there was no Rory…

It had already happened—once with Rory and once with Peter. Why were all the men in her life deceitful? Could she not be attracted to anything but lies?

No, it was better to keep her guard up. Trust no one and she wouldn't get hurt.

"Mommy!" Nicky exclaimed, waving a piece of paper in the air. "Look at what I just won!"

It was a certificate for a free throw at the dunking booth. "You won this playing darts?"

"No. A boy came up to me and gave it to me just now. He said I won it."

Maddie shrugged and smiled at her son. "Must be some sort of door prize. C'mon, kiddo. Let's go dunk somebody."

Nicky saw Rory at the exact same moment that Maddie did. She wanted to turn and run, but knew it was too late for that. Her gaze met Rory's, and her heart flamed to life even as she realized that this must be some sort of setup.

"Excuse me," she said to the wet-haired woman behind the counter, "but could you please tell me how many of these door prizes you've handed out today?"

"There are no door prizes," the woman said, but firmly plucked the certificate from Maddie's hand nevertheless. "Give the boy a round of balls," she called to the operator.

Maddie had been conned again, and the familiar flush of anger replaced the warmth pervading her heart.

The sign stuck to the side of the booth confirmed it: Dunk Neil March, Owner of March's Department Store.

Boy, would she like to dunk *him*.

"It's the Fireman!" Nicky exclaimed, waving at Rory.

Rory smiled and waved back to the boy. He looked genuinely happy, dangling his stockinged feet off the edge of a makeshift diving board and calling friendly taunts to Nicky. Maddie felt her throat constrict, then quickly repressed the emotion with another surge of anger.

Anger, she found, was stronger than her less predictable emotions, and right now she needed all the bolstering she could get.

His white-blond hair falling loosely over his

forehead, Nicky took the first of three balls, aimed carefully and let loose.

It dropped just short of the target.

"You missed me, sport. But I'll bet I take a dive next time around!" Rory called cheerfully. "C'mon, big guy. Throw me that ball!"

Nicky, his brow furrowed in concentration, threw the second ball high and to the left. His shoulders slumped in defeat. "Aw, I can't do this," he mumbled.

Maddie's heart tightened at her son's fallen look. "It's okay, Nicky. You don't have to throw that last ball if you don't want to."

"Yes. He does," Rory said from the platform, his dark eyes boring into hers.

"Who asked you?" she snapped, aware of the crowd lingering around the booth.

"Nicky, pick up the ball." Rory's voice was low but forceful, and the boy immediately obeyed.

Maddie felt her blood pressure rise, until she was certain that she must have steam escaping from her ears. How *dare* the man override her instructions to her son? How *dare* he believe that he knew what was best for Nicky?

Now Nicky would be hurt and Neil March was to blame.

So what was new? The man had a distinct talent for ruining her life. She shot him a mind-your-own-business glare and crossed her arms over her chest.

Waiting. Watching.

"Now here's the thing, sport," Rory instructed quietly. "You don't have to win, but you do have to try. So give that third throw all you've got, and either way you'll be a winner."

Nicky wiped the frown from his face and nodded at Rory. "Yes, sir!"

Maddie felt a cloud of self-doubt hover over her. Suddenly she could see herself as if from a distance, stepping in to play the protective mother hen when what her son really needed was a man's advice, a chance to prove himself.

It's not whether you win or lose, but how you play the game. A wise old adage Maddie would have completely ignored had Rory not stepped in.

She was always the one calling "Be careful!" to her tree-climbing son, while Peter had always hollered "How high can you climb?"

Not that one was better than the other, she mentally amended. A boy needed both. But now, with only his mother giving counsel, he was being coddled, however unintentionally.

She was sheltering him from real life. Over-protecting him when what he really needed was a firm push forward. Like Rory was giving him now.

Nicky took aim and let loose, slamming the ball into the target.

With a whoop, Rory went into the pool, hollering nearly as loudly as was Nicky until his head was submerged.

"Did you see that, Mom? I did it!" Nicky exclaimed, hugging Maddie around the waist and dancing her around.

"Yes, you did!" she agreed, trying to gently wriggle herself free from her son's overenthusiastic embrace.

Rory stood, shaking the water out of his face with a flick of his head. "Way to go, sport! See what can happen if you just keep trying?"

Over Nicky's head, Maddie met Rory's flaming gaze and her heartbeat quickened. His gaze always affected her like that, and she wondered why no one else seemed to notice the way his eyes blazed, how he spoke volumes with those obsidian orbs.

She sent him a silent "thank you," which he acknowledged with a nod. Not a smug or

I-told-you-so gesture, but a simple nod of acceptance mixed with a trace of gratitude.

Maddie wondered what he had to be grateful for. He was now sopping wet, and she doubted that he had a change of clothes. It was freezing outside. He was bound to catch a cold, if not something worse.

Oh, what do I care, she scolded herself. But in her heart she knew she did care. Very much.

"Your turn," Rory said, causing her to jerk from her thoughts. She coughed to dislodge the lump in her throat. With his dark hair slicked back, his bold features looked more compelling than she could ever have imagined.

She found herself gaping at Rory like a teenager in love with a rock star. She hoped the trail of her thoughts hadn't been obvious to others, especially to Rory, but from the glimmer of laughter in his eyes, she doubted her luck in *that* department.

"What?" she asked in dismay. He was staring at her, and was clearly amused by what he saw. He cocked a dark wet eyebrow, the ghost of a smile hovering on his lips.

"I said—" Rory tossed a softball at her "—it's your turn."

His eyes darkened and his smile disappeared. Suddenly it was no game they played, but what felt like a battle—a battle between two strong wills.

"Do it, Maddie." His eyes challenged her, a smirk of amusement in the corner of his mouth giving her every reason in the world to want to knock it off with a softball.

And she was good. Very good. He had no way of knowing that. She was the pitcher on her church softball league. And she could hit the smirk right off his face if she wanted to.

But that's what he wanted her to do. And because it was his game, she no longer wanted to play. Or at least that's what she told herself as she felt her cheeks warm with embarrassment.

People—complete strangers—were laughing and staring at her, caught up in her bickering with Rory and apparently waiting for her to do who-knew-what with the softball.

As if she would stoop to such a juvenile level as to dunk Rory in the pool, worthy of that honor though he might be. An *ice* pool, if she had her way.

But there was nothing on earth that could convince her to play Rory's game. She was not about to give in to aka Neil March. She tossed the softball on the counter with what she hoped was an aloof flick of her hand. "I'm fresh out of tickets."

Rory's eyebrows set in a line over his eyes, which had darkened to midnight-black. "It's free today."

"Not for me, it's not," Maddie countered, her voice squeaking from the catch in her throat. "Come on, Nicky, let's go home."

Nicky, who was swinging the plastic base-ball bat he'd won from dunking Rory, groaned in protest.

"You want to see your mom try to dunk me, don't you, sport?" Rory asked, summoning his reinforcements.

"Yeah, Mom. Do it!"

"Yeah, Mom," Rory repeated with a grim smile, "do it."

She glared at him, but he matched her stare for stare, refusing to blink, move or otherwise break away. How *dare* he pit her son against her that way? What was the man's problem, anyway?

"Are you afraid to try?" He singsonged through a line of "Scaredy-Cat," his eyes gleaming as he intentionally broke their eye contact.

He was trying to provoke her, and in front

of strangers, no less! She clenched her fists, fighting to maintain the fine line of control that kept her from diving over the counter and dunking him personally.

She took a deep, steadying breath. His ploy wasn't going to work. She was good and mad, but she wouldn't be manipulated into a water fight. Especially not in front of people she didn't know.

"You couldn't hit the side of a barn. Your aim is so bad you probably couldn't hit me if I were right in front of your nose."

Watch me, you bag of hot air. She eyed him as he took his seat on the latched board and began flutter-kicking the water at his feet.

Juvenile. Infantile. She rolled her eyes. *Sticks and stones and all that stuff,* she reminded her right hand, which curled around a softball on the counter.

Just one throw. That's all it would take to knock that windbag off his perch. And oh, would that feel good.

She gripped the ball and fought for control. Part of her really wanted to take him out. An almost irresistible part of her.

But she wouldn't play his game. She wouldn't. No matter what he called her.

Her eyes locked with his as she set the ball on the counter with a thud, then brushed her hands together in the universal gesture of completion. Finally, forcing a smile that didn't reach her heart, she turned away from him.

He chuckled. "If that isn't just like a woman. Turn and run. Give up before you even start. I didn't peg you as a quitter, but hey, you win some, you lose some. And some games you don't even have the guts to play."

She tensed at his words. Give up? Maddie Carlton, *give up?*

Not in this lifetime.

She had fought a galaxy of battles in the past year. She'd won some, and had come perilously close to losing others.

But she never, *ever* quit.

She whirled so quickly that she couldn't focus on the counter, never mind the target, but nonetheless her hand made contact with a softball. The crowds faded to a dull outline of faces and colors as she scooped the ball into her grasp.

Without even bothering to aim, she slung her arm with every bit of her strength. And missed the mark completely. She hadn't even hit the background, but had sent the ball flying pell-mell into the side of the tent.

Rory had the gall to laugh. "Told you. I knew you couldn't throw a ball."

"Yeah?" Maddie ground out. "Watch me." Her anger was rushing in spurts down her arm, giving her extra throwing power. She knew she could hit the target, and she coaxed herself to relax as she pulled her arm back for another try.

The ball hit the target with a refreshing clang of metal.

"Yes!" She punched a fist of triumph in the air as the man dropped sprawling into the water.

He came up sputtering and laughing. "Not bad. For a girl." He swiped a hand down his face. In moments he had reset the latch and was climbing back on the board. "Now do it again."

As if summoned by a force beyond her control, fury consumed her. She snatched a ball from a waiting attendant and hurled it at the target.

This one's for you, Neil March! her mind screamed as the ball once again made contact with the target and dumped the shivering man into the water.

She didn't even question it when Rory rose from the water and said, "Again."

She grabbed another softball and threw it at the target. Her insides were burning, her head pounding. She was no longer cognizant of the people gathered around the booth, or even of the dripping, dark-eyed man. She only knew her anger, her frustration.

Her pain.

The pounding fury subsided as quickly as it had come, leaving her weak-kneed and breathing heavily. Dazed, she staggered away, leaving Nicky to help Rory towel his clothes off at the front of the booth. She found a quiet place to slump to the floor, leaning her back against a wall.

Her heart fluttered in her throat as her blood pressure returned to normal.

She began to shiver, her body shaking so hard that her teeth chattered. As if *she* had been the one repeatedly dumped into a pool of ice water.

But it wasn't a chill that was making her quake. Maddie recognized the hard knot in her stomach…the queasiness making her head spin…for what it was.

She was frightened. Of herself.

It wasn't Neil March and his deceit that she had been lashing out at as she'd thrown those balls in fury. It wasn't even Peter, who had abandoned her with his death.

No, neither man was the object of her wrath.

Chapter Eleven

The cold gray marble headstone shimmered in the morning mist. Maddie wrapped her parka more firmly around her waist and dropped to her knees beside the well-tended grave. With trembling fingers, she reached out and touched the engraving, fingering the letters almost as if reading braille: Peter Carlton. Faithful Husband. Loving Father.

The words burned into her heart. She hadn't chosen the inscription, couldn't have instructed what she considered a bald-faced lie to be carved indelibly into the marble reminder of Peter's existence.

It was enough to make the old hurt start showing through. Today, though, she didn't feel like crying, at least not in pain. A few *angry* tears might fall before the day was through.

"I met someone," she said aloud, glancing around the vacant cemetery to make certain that she was alone. She didn't want others to hear her. She'd made enough of a spectacle of herself over the past two weeks to last a lifetime. And Rory March was the cause of it all.

No, that wasn't right, either. She'd been placing blame anywhere she could to keep from dealing with her grief. Peter. Neil March. Even God. But now she realized she'd made a choice, however unconscious, to fly a holding pattern, to avoid anything that might cause her pain. Ironically, she'd ended up being hurt more from hiding than from facing life head-on.

Now, more than anything, she wanted her life back. She was determined to end the pity party and confront whatever she needed to confront.

And the first place her resolution had taken her was to Peter's grave. She'd asked her mother to watch Nicky so that she might have some time alone, time to visit Peter. The two of them had unfinished business between them. And she wanted to say the words aloud.

She arranged the assortment of roses she had brought about the headstone, a shock of red and white against the dreary gray backdrop.

When she finished, she sat back on her heels, observing her work.

"His name is Rory." The name sounded so sweet on her lips that she said it again. "Rory."

She stood and brushed dirt from the knees of her blue jeans. Her heart lapped calmly like waves against the shore. She wondered at the way even the thought of Rory could bring such peace. And yet such turmoil. His gentle smile made her feel safe, secure. But his dark, flashing eyes made her heart leap wildly.

Had Peter ever evoked such polar reactions? All she could remember was the hurt, the anger. There had been a time when she'd fancied herself in love, and maybe what she felt for Peter *was* love. But it was certainly different from what she felt for Rory.

"He's nothing like you." It sounded like an accusation. Maddie was surprised by her own bitter tone. Time had erased at least some of the pain, but too much still lurked just underneath the surface.

She closed her eyes and willed Peter's image into her mind. He had been tall, lithe and very blond. But at this very moment, try as she might, his face remained a blur.

In some ways it was a welcome blur, but another part of her wanted to panic. Peter's memory was all she had left of him. And though they had been arguing before he died, their life together hadn't always been that way.

Once upon a time, they'd promised each other the world, shared the same youthful idealism, their hopes and dreams for the future. Peter had been cocky and sure of himself, and Maddie had thought the world turned on his smile. She would have risked anything for his love. She did, in fact, throw her own career choices away to pursue *his* dreams.

At the time it hadn't seemed such a great sacrifice. Now...

Now she was alone with a son to support. Much as she hated to admit it, if it weren't for Neil March's money, they might have starved.

No. That wasn't true. Maddie might not have a college education, but she was determined, and a determined woman couldn't be stopped. She would have made a life for her son even without March's blood money.

She plucked a delicate red rose from the arrangement, looking blankly at her finger when a thorn pierced her skin, causing a tiny droplet of blood to fall on her jeans.

Slowly she began picking the petals from the flower, one by one.

He loves me. He loves me not.

The children's game jumped unbidden to her mind, and her shoulders tensed. "Did you love me?" she whispered at the headstone. "Did you ever love me, Peter?"

How well she remembered walking down the aisle to become his bride. He had been so happy then, so proud to have her on his arm, to call her his wife.

They'd been young. Full of dreams. But like most young couples, life hadn't been the carefree ride they had anticipated. Bills began to mount. Peter wasn't able to pursue his dream of owning his own tax firm. Instead, he worked indecent hours for ridiculously small wages, caught in the vicious trap of middle management, left with nowhere to go, no ladder of success to climb.

He'd become bitter. Angry. He never complained, but Maddie knew he hated his job, and resented her for tying him down.

The man who used to burst in the door with humorous stories about his day began dragging in after hours, flopping on the couch in front of a blaring television. Not willing to share his day. Never asking about hers.

And then she'd discovered she was pregnant. Nicky had been an accident that she had soon seen as a blessing. The intimacy she lacked with Peter, she found in Nicky, and her son became the center of her world.

She and Peter had drawn further and further apart. To Peter, Nicky had represented another ball and chain, another bleak responsibility keeping him from his dreams. Maddie had resented Peter's attitude and had become withdrawn, distant.

And he'd sought comfort elsewhere. She'd seen it with her own eyes. Peter meeting a woman over lunch. Laughing with her. Whispering to her and sharing secrets that had once been for Maddie's ears alone.

She'd strained to see the face of this nameless woman, but she'd been too far away, and the woman's back had been turned toward Maddie. Instead, she lived with the memory of Peter's joy-filled face as he looked at the other woman.

Her thoughts snapped back to the present with all the ferocity of a bullwhip. The past was past. She couldn't change what had happened, however much she might wish she could. Perhaps if she'd been more understanding...

But it was too late for that. It was time to face the future.

Peter's death had been the key that locked her in, trapping her in the past with nothing but her memories for company.

Rory had changed all that. She had no trouble bringing *his* face to mind: the dominant chin, strong cheekbones and aquiline nose. His piercing black eyes and charming, ready smile.

That smile had broken her prison doors wide-open, allowed her to see the future. To laugh again. To live again.

Her heart swelled as she plucked the final petal from the rose stem. "He loves me," she whispered, and smiled.

She turned toward her car, then stopped abruptly and turned back toward the marble headstone. "And I," she said clearly, her voice sounding like the lilting tinkle of a bell on the wind, "just may love him, too."

Chapter Twelve

Maddie stuffed a handful of popcorn in her mouth and slid farther down into the chair, her eyes never leaving the movie screen. She could feel Rory's eyes on her, but she'd intentionally chosen a seat between two strangers. She didn't want to chance being alone with Rory.

Above all, she didn't want to be alone with herself. Her house—once a safe haven, a fortress to keep others out—now felt like a huge trash compactor. The walls were closing in on her, and there was no one to trigger the release.

After seeing Nicky off to school each morning, she tried to lose herself. She wanted to be where there were crowds. The noisier, the better.

Anything to drown out her thoughts. She spent an extra half hour in the morning reading the Bible, trying to find answers to her dilemma.

Until that day at the dunking booth, she had thought her biggest problems were her hatred of Neil March and her inability to deal with Peter's death. But she had no idea that she possessed the kind of violent emotion that had displayed itself that day. It was black, and ugly, and she didn't want to dwell on it.

As if that weren't bad enough, her conflicting feelings for Rory March never left her whirling mind. It was too much to sort out. She wished she could just forget about it for a while—take a vacation from her thoughts.

But that, she discovered, was impossible, thanks to Rory. Everywhere she went, he was there: the dry cleaner's, the grocery store, even the bank. He was tailing her like a bodyguard—never speaking to her, but never letting her out of his sight. Just when she would feel the comfort of being lost in a crowd, she'd sense that dark gaze on her, and her distress would begin once again.

For all she knew, he had staked out her house. The man must never sleep, she thought. It didn't matter what time of day or night she tried to seek a few minutes' respite from the agony of her thoughts... Rory was there.

He never tried to approach her, but his continued presence was like a thorn in her side. She couldn't deal with Rory yet. She couldn't even deal with herself, and she had a lifetime's worth of baggage to unload before she could begin to consider what to do with Mr. Neil Rory March III.

This afternoon, she had wanted to take in a movie, some gut-wrenching sob story. The cover of darkness was tempting. She'd be able to hide there, lose herself and her problems.

Or so she thought. But Rory's gaze pierced into her back from his seat directly behind her. Even without turning around, she knew he was there, could feel him watching her. Reaching out to her.

And she wasn't ready. What's more, she was sick and tired of trying to avoid him.

She hadn't the slightest idea what the movie was about, though she'd been staring at the screen for a good half hour. That was Rory's fault, too.

"I've had it." She turned and whispered at Rory, momentarily forgetting her usual rule not to make a scene in front of strangers. "You're driving me crazy."

He grinned, as if he were pleased.

Would the man never learn? He was the most incorrigible human being she'd ever had the misfortune to know. "Now, you listen, and listen good. I'm walking out of this theater, and if you so much as *budge* from that seat, you're going to regret it."

He cocked an amused eyebrow. "That so?"

"That's *so,*" she affirmed, punctuating her sentence by dumping half a bucket of popcorn on his lap. "Besides, you've got a mess to clean up."

Without waiting for his reaction, she spun away from him and marched up the aisle toward the exit, ignoring the applause and catcalls from amused patrons. Anger burned on her cheeks. And that was *all* it was. She wouldn't let herself be embarrassed for putting Rory in his place. The man deserved what he got and more.

There must be somewhere she could hide from both Rory and her feelings at the same time, she thought as she stepped out into the sunlight. But where would he *not* go?

A women's health club? Maybe. But Maddie didn't feel like working out. And knowing Rory, he'd think nothing of bursting into the women's locker room and demanding her attention. Especially after what she'd just done to him.

Penelope's. Of course! Why hadn't she thought of that sooner? Neil March would never dare set foot in his greatest rival's department store.

She would go to the mall and shop until she dropped, comfortably surrounded by the humming mill of Christmas shoppers. She would forget about Rory, and herself, for a while. And she would use Neil March's money to do it.

Funny, but it was easier to spend the money now that she knew it was Rory's. *His* money didn't seem as tarnished as the elusive Neil March's.

A glance at her watch told her it was time to pick Nicky up from school. Perfect. They'd make a day of it, maybe take in a burger and a thick, chocolate milk shake afterward. And Nicky hadn't been to see Santa yet. Tonight would be the perfect night.

She could finish up her Christmas shopping, spend quality time with her son and escape her nagging conscience—all in one fell swoop.

"When are we gonna see Santa?" Nicky asked the moment she pulled her car into Eastlake Mall. The two anchor stores for the mall were Penelope's and March's. There was absolutely no way Rory would follow her into the competing store with his own store weighing in at the other end, she reassured her quavering heart. Not when he might be recognized. He probably knew Penelope personally.

"Soon, Nicky," she said, adjusting the boy's hood over his head to protect him from the frigid wind. "I have a bit of shopping to do first."

And a bit of forgetting. She would need more than a shopping expedition to erase a lifetime of hurt. But it was a start.

With an occasional furtive glance backward, she crossed the parking lot with Nicky in tow. She half expected Rory to tackle her in the lot, or at least to hover near the entrance, those dark, speaking eyes of his making her feel guilty for shopping the competition.

But there was no sign of him.

With an audible sigh, she relaxed, the tension draining from her shoulders. When her heart tugged gently in disappointment, she ignored it, refusing to analyze the significance.

Rory was a heavy burden to bear when she had so much else on her mind. Her feelings for him were becoming more and more obvious. The harder she tried to fight, the stronger they insisted on being heard.

She *had* to force Rory from her mind—at least until she'd dealt with the other issues haunting her. She couldn't go on with her life unless she closed the chapter on her past. But was she really ready to do that? Could she face her suspicions and forgive Peter for what he might or might not have done—for the fact that he'd deserted her, just as her father had once done? Could she honestly forgive and forget?

She didn't know the answer to any of those questions, and her head was beginning to ache from thinking about it.

She sorted through a row of boy's pajamas, looking for Nicky's favorite cartoon characters.

"You'll get a far better deal at March's," advised a deep voice from behind her left shoulder, the rich vibrancy of his tone sending a tendril of delight up her spine.

A chocolate voice, Maddie thought. Smooth and rich. A voice that could make her knees turn to jelly and her heartbeat skip erratically.

"Rory, what are you doing here?" she demanded, spinning to face him.

"You really should shop around, you know. You'll save a good dollar on that product at my store." He made a sweeping gesture with his hand. "Come to think of it, I don't know why you're in Penelope's at all. Take it from someone who knows—everything in this place is overpriced and understocked."

"I came here to get away from you," Maddie said bluntly, unable to contain the jolt of her heart when he crooked a smile.

He placed a hand over his heart. "You wound me. And here I thought you were getting fond of this ugly mug of mine."

Maddie nearly laughed aloud. Ugly mug, indeed. Rory March's striking good looks would stand out in any crowd, the puckered scar on his temple notwithstanding.

But it was his compassionate, dark eyes that attracted her most. Especially when they burned as they were when he looked at her as he was doing now. As if she were the only woman in the world. As if he were right where he wanted to be. By her side. She felt alive. Attractive. The way he had made her feel the night they met.

Put a clamp on it, she reminded herself harshly. He'll only hurt you.

"Don't you have someplace to be?" she snapped, angry with herself at how easily she capitulated.

Taking her gently by the shoulders, he leaned in until his mouth was brushing her earlobe. "Only with you."

Her blood was pulsating so rapidly through her limbs she was certain Rory could feel it in her shoulders. She made a pretense of guiding Nicky down the toy aisle, using the time to reel in her whimsical emotions. "Aren't you afraid Penelope will see you?" she asked, seeing that Rory remained at her elbow.

He barked out a laugh. "Penelope has a plush office in LoDo. I don't think she's even *been* to this store. Except maybe for a press conference or something."

Maddie chewed the side of her lip. "Oh." There went her small-town, middle-class roots showing themselves again. Silly her, to imagine the owner of a store might actually *work* there. She felt like a fool, and couldn't contain the betraying blush rushing to her face.

Neil noticed the color that stained her cheeks a kissable pink. "I'm not laughing at you, Maddie," he said quietly, hoping to reassure her. "I work in *my* store. I believe that I shouldn't ask my employees to do anything I'm not willing to do myself, and that goes all the way down to putting up displays and taking out the trash."

"Oh," said Maddie again, looking small, and vulnerable, and absolutely adorable. Neil wanted to wrap her in his arms and promise her that she'd never be hurt again.

Instead, he reached out a finger to stroke her cheek. To his surprise, she didn't pull away, though he felt her jaw tense at his touch. He continued his monologue in an effort to distract her. "It's a sound business philosophy. March's has a reputation for low employee turnover. Almost unheard of in retail."

Her eyes widened and she pulled away from his hand. Neil shoved his hands in his pockets to keep from reaching for her. The need to touch her, to comfort her, was almost overwhelming, but he knew she would run if he touched her again. She was as skittish as a kitten. And with good reason. She had every right to want to run from him.

"Penelope, on the other hand," he continued, trying to hold her with his words, "wouldn't be caught dead in her store, never mind doing menial labor. She might break a nail."

"Oh."

He could see a question in her eyes, but she remained silent. "What is it, Maddie?" he asked gently.

She spoke so quietly that he almost didn't hear her words. "I can't shop in March's. I can't go back in there."

The pain in her words lanced him. Like her, he had memories haunting him, but he had been able to overcome them, to rebuild. Or at least to pretend that he had.

Something she was obviously not ready to do.

"I wasn't thinking," he apologized tightly. "Of course you'd feel uncomfortable there."

He turned and strode off, afraid to look back, afraid of what he would see written on Maddie's countenance. Every time he made progress, his past would slap him in the face. It was always there, hovering in the background, waiting to jump out if Neil got too close.

And it would always be there. He'd done everything he could think of to make things right, but it obviously wasn't enough. He was made to endure continued torture, the noose around his neck tightening slowly, choking the life out of him.

What did God expect of him? He thrust his fingers through the curls at his neck, attempting to massage away the lines of tension shooting darts into his head.

He'd do it—whatever *it* was—if he could be with Maddie.

He had to be with Maddie.

"Mr. March!" Jason approached wearing a frantic expression. He took Neil by the arm as he exited Penelope's and entered the mall. "We've been looking all over for you!"

Surprised, Neil allowed Jason to lead him down the mall.

"Are you going to tell me what this is all about?" he asked, humor underlying his tone, "or am I supposed to guess? Offhand," he continued, glancing down at the viselike hold Jason had on his upper arm, "I'd have to guess it must involve some sort of emergency."

Jason's face reddened under his mop of brown curls and he dropped his hold on Neil. "I beg your pardon, sir," he apologized with a groan that indicated he'd realized he'd overstepped his boundaries.

"No offense taken," Neil assured his young secretary.

"It's just that, well, sir, you're late for your appointment as—"

Jason's words were cut off by the approach of the store's publicity agent, Pattie. "It's about time you showed up, Santa. Your stint begins in five minutes. Not a lot of time to get into your suit."

"Santa?" Neil repeated with a blank look.

"Surely you didn't forget you promised the mall to play Santa for some much-needed publicity? Something to distract people from remembering the fire?"

He took a deep breath, then slowly released it. The last thing he wanted right now was to be surrounded by crowds and cameras. "Reschedule," he said, sounding more gruff than he'd intended.

"I'm sorry, sir, but we can't do that. It's too close to Christmas and the press is already here in droves."

Neil rubbed a hand across his pounding forehead. "Then cancel."

He turned to walk away when Pattie's words stopped him short.

"You'll be responsible for disappointing all

those children, then? You'll give them a year with no Santa?"

With a sigh, he turned around. "Oh, for crying out loud. Bring on the beard and the big red suit."

Pattie's frown turned to a luminous smile. "I knew it. I just knew it."

Minutes later, Jason was adjusting the belt around Neil's red-clad, pillow-stuffed waist. Fortunately, he thought wryly, the fluffy white beard that covered his cheeks and chin also hid his scar. He didn't want his scars to scare any of the children.

"Hmm," Jason mumbled with a frown, putting the finishing touches on Neil's beard. "This thing won't stay straight."

"Leave it," Neil replied.

Pattie took a step back and looked him over, from the tip of his fur-trimmed cap to the toes of his black boots.

He struggled not to squirm under her inspection, which made him feel like a first-grade kid on class picture day.

"Yes, I think you'll do very nicely," she said at last, tapping her fingers on her chin. "Quite nicely indeed."

Neil looked down at his blaring red, portly figure and grinned. "I'm not certain I agree."

Her blond eyebrows puckered. "You may be right. Let's hear it."

"Hear...what?" Neil croaked, wishing he'd left good enough alone.

"Why your laugh, of course. Give me something loud and jovial. Deep and hearty. Oh, and don't forget to shake your stomach like a bowl full of jelly."

He was getting acting lessons. Santa acting lessons from a totally serious and professional female executive? He couldn't help but burst out laughing.

She shook her head vigorously. "No, no! That's not it at all. My word, do I have to coach you on your lines, as well? The correct version is 'Ho, ho, ho.' I hope you can remember that."

"Ho, ho, ho," Neil repeated, tempering her sarcasm with his own blandness. "I think I can remember that."

"You'd better." Then she turned him around by the shoulders and, with an audible grunt, pushed him out of the dressing room and into a mall packed with waiting children.

"Santa! It's Santa!" a young girl exclaimed, enthusiastically tugging on Neil's pant leg.

Moments later he was surrounded by children of all ages and their harried-looking parents. Some of the younger kids clamored for his attention, latching their fists on to his clothing or shyly holding his hand.

One preteen boy even attempted to yank on his beard, but Neil deftly maneuvered himself out of the boy's grasp.

Stifling an un-Santa-like laugh, he looked back for his publicity elf's assistance, but she was nowhere to be seen.

"Ho, ho, ho," he bellowed, doing his best to sound robust, as much for Pattie, wherever she had disappeared to, as for the children who howled in delight when he spoke.

He knew Eastlake Mall intimately from his many years at March's, so he began moving toward the sleigh in the center of the mall that usually held Santa Claus.

It was slow going, with children attached to each leg and everyone talking at once. He was immediately taken in by the eager innocence in the children's adoring gazes.

He could almost remember a time when he believed in Santa Claus himself. But it wasn't that reminiscence that stung him.

He'd been about Nicky's age, if memory

served, when his wisecracking father had spilled the beans and left a devastated six-year-old boy vowing never to believe in anyone again.

Not Santa. Not his father. Not even Jesus.

The only one he could believe in was himself.

Neil's throat tightened. He didn't know exactly how he had come to play Santa Claus in the chaos he called a life. But whatever the reason, he was determined to be the best Santa Claus the media, the mall and the children, had ever seen.

Chapter Thirteen

"Now, Mom?" Nicky asked for the twentieth time in as many minutes.

Maddie glanced at her watch. Had Rory been gone for twenty minutes? It seemed an eternity.

Out of sight, out of mind. Oh, if only it were that easy. But for Maddie, Rory's being out of sight only meant that he plagued her mind, not that he left her in peace. Where was he? What was he doing? And why was he no longer following her around?

He'd been her constant shadow for weeks. And now he had disappeared. That she'd given him the royal brush-off was beside the point. He'd never taken the hint before. Why now?

And why was she feeling anxious rather than relieved? She'd come here to escape Rory, after all. But somehow being alone seemed worse than having Rory's gaze perpetually upon her.

"Yeah, sure, honey. We can go see Santa Claus." And then go home. A steaming bubble bath was definitely in order. Maybe a long soak and a good book would rid her mind of her pesky Phantom.

The line for Santa was unusually long, curling around the back side of the display.

Maddie sighed. It would be a long wait, and she was tired, emotionally as much as physically. "Do you want a soda or something before we get in line?" she asked her son.

Nicky shook his head vigorously and pointed to the display. "Look, Mom. Reindeer!"

The glistening cotton snow and the mechanical elves, reindeer and forest creatures looked so much like March's display that it gave Maddie shivers. She slanted a look at her son, wondering if he noticed the resemblance. But he was leaning far over the rail, his little arms flailing in a futile attempt to touch the bobbing head of the nearest reindeer. Apparently, that part of his past was forgotten. Just as well forgotten, as far as Maddie was concerned. The less poor Nicky had to remember and suffer, the better.

She pointed out a bunny and raccoon wrapping a present, and listened with half an ear as he exclaimed over the display, glad that she could give him back the childhood joy of Christmas.

She only wished she could give herself the same simple happiness. But she wasn't as pliable as she'd been as a child. She still harbored too many doubts to be truly happy. This year, her son's happiness would have to be enough for her.

The couple in front of her bounced a chubby infant between them. The tiny girl was, Maddie noticed with a small flutter of her heart, dressed for the season in a green velvet gown, shiny black shoes and an adorable curly bow fastened to a lock of downy black hair.

Maddie smiled, wondering not for the first time what it would be like to have a daughter of her own. Someone to dress up, do up her hair, share jewelry with. A little girl who would play with Maddie's makeup and who would want to emulate Mommy.

Her throat caught around the scratchy feeling of welling emotion. She'd always wanted more children. She and Peter had planned to have another baby when the time was right, but with Peter's work schedule and the demands placed on Maddie by her rambunctious son, that time never came.

And now it never would.

Bittersweet longing filled her. The baby girl was so precious, even when she went from gurgling and cooing to fussing and fuming. And she shared the turmoil of the small girl's parents who, embarrassed by their baby's wailing, tried a pacifier, and then a bottle in an attempt to soothe her. Nothing seemed to quiet the girl, not even being steadily rocked in her mother's arms.

Maddie recognized the desperate look that passed between the parents as, without words, they struggled to decide whether or not to keep their place in the line, which was getting slowly shorter. She remembered when Nicky had been that age, how helpless she had felt when he refused to respond to her gentle care.

Finally, the tiny girl stopped wailing and settled in her mother's arms. The baby's father tickled and cooed and made silly faces until he brought a dimpled smile to his daughter's face. Just in time for Santa.

"Ho, ho, ho."

Maddie's spine stiffened at the familiar rich

baritone, and she whirled to see what could not possibly be true, but which was instantly confirmed. Her gaze met Santa's warm, dark eyes.

Rory March was playing Santa Claus.

And it was far too late for Maddie to back out now. If the long line of anxious children and parents thought the wailing baby had been loud, it was nothing to the uproar Nicky would make should she choose to drag him kicking and screaming out of the mall without seeing Santa. A six-year-old boy could throw fits that could put a baby's fussing to shame.

Besides, she *wanted* Nicky to see Santa— to put to rest any nightmares that lingered in his dreams. He had to move beyond his fear if he was to heal completely. That meant seeing Santa Claus, even if the jolly old elf happened to be Rory March. She'd just have to deal with it the best she could, for her son's sake and that alone. She would not, she reminded her fluttering heart, allow herself to get flustered over the man. Even if he did look adorable as Santa Claus.

The baby in front of them renewed her screaming fit the moment she laid eyes on the plump, bearded stranger reaching for her. The girl's mom looked mortified. Her dad wore a frustrated scowl, looking as if he was ready to snatch the fussy baby from Santa's arms and forget the whole thing.

And Santa? Rory looked…

Happy.

She'd seen his eyes light up with joy before, and there was no mistaking the pleasure he was taking from his role.

With soft, calm words he quieted the baby, bouncing her gently on one of his red-clad knees. He didn't get her to stop crying, but at least he was able to tone the decibels down a few notches.

He took immediate control with the gentle authority that was so completely Rory, suggesting the mother crouch down by her child for the photo.

With a wavering smile of gratitude, she complied, kneeling by Santa's side and putting a comforting hand around her daughter. The infant, seeing her mother comfortable with the stranger, became excited and began babbling, eventually cracking a smile that was quickly snapped by the waiting photographer-elf. As Rory smiled for the camera, looking as if he played Santa every day of the week, Maddie had no trouble speculating why he volunteered for the job.

If that's what it was…. For all she knew, the mall required its store owners to take turns as Santa.

Whatever misplaced sense of philanthropy led Rory to don the red suit and play the jolly old elf, watching him in action was another blatant reminder that Rory March was not the coldhearted playboy she once believed him to be.

He gave of *himself*—not just his money or his time.

And he liked children.

"Next!" the efficient little photographer-elf announced in a singsong voice.

Nicky bounded up the stairs, then came to a dead halt, his eyes wide and glistening before the bearded stranger. His bottom lip began quivering as his eyes met Santa's, and even the man's jolly "Ho, ho, ho" didn't wipe the look of distress from the boy's face.

Maddie stood, wavering, uncertain of what to do. How could she rescue her son without damaging his fragile little-boy ego and embarrassing him in front of strangers? How could she let him know that he wasn't facing his fear alone, that his mother's heart was with him every step of the way?

Nicky was oblivious to his surroundings, his attention focused completely on Santa. His eyes darted to the cotton snow behind and around him, and then back to Santa and all he represented.

Then he turned and ran back to Maddie, hugging her legs and burying his face in her stomach. Tamping down her own emotions to respond to her son's anguish, she gently placed an arm around his shoulders and stroked the back of his head with her other hand, murmuring soft words of encouragement.

She hazarded a glance at Rory, who returned her look of concern. She thought he might try to approach the boy, but he remained seated, his brow furrowed and his hands gripping the armrests of his chair.

When Nicky shivered, she dropped to one knee and cupped his chin with her palm. "What's wrong?" she whispered for his ears only. "I thought you *wanted* to see Santa Claus."

Nicky nodded vigorously, tears making his big blue eyes shine in a way that nearly broke Maddie's heart.

She bit her tongue to keep from asking him

if he was scared. Of course he was scared. He was in just such a display when he lost his father. But how could she help him get over the trauma?

Her mind spun, examining and discarding option after option, while an impatient crowd began to murmur behind her. Whatever action she chose, it would have to be fast.

"Santa took my daddy away," Nicky admitted, his bottom lip resuming its heart-wrenching quiver.

"Oh, Nicky, no!" Maddie exclaimed, hugging her son to her chest. "No. Santa Claus didn't take your father away. Santa is a good man. He brings toys and gifts to good little children, remember?"

Nicky frowned and shook his head furiously.

She knew Rory could hear their conversation. The pained look in his eyes was a clear indication that he was hurting right along with Nicky.

"It was an accident, son," Maddie continued, struggling to keep her voice reassuringly calm. "Nobody is to blame, especially not Santa Claus."

Nicky's mouth twisted as he considered her words.

Rory gestured with his white-gloved hands. He wanted her to come to him—for them to come to him. Compassion filled his gaze, and suddenly Maddie was glad Santa had turned out to be Rory March.

She tried another tactic, hoping to convince her son to give Santa a chance to redeem himself. It was a tall order, but if anyone could do the job, it would be Rory. Maddie sent up a silent prayer of thanks.

"Maybe you can ask him for something really special this Christmas. To make up for last Christmas, you know?" At least she could do that much for her son, thanks to Rory's money.

"Anything?" Nicky asked, his eyes beginning to sparkle with enthusiasm.

Maddie chuckled. "Well, almost anything. I don't think Santa will bring you a car. At least not for another ten years or so."

Nicky smiled and nodded. "I know what I want."

"Great!" she said, encouraged by his eagerness. "Do you think you can tell Santa Claus about it?"

Nicky eyed Santa with a combination of suspicion and reverence, then nodded. He took a step forward but faltered, looking back at his mother. "Can you come with me? Please?"

Maddie looked up at Rory, who smiled back at her. "Sure, honey. I can come with you if you want me to."

Taking her son's hand, she marched him up the stairs. Rory held out his hands to Nicky. The boy slid a glance to Maddie, who nodded her encouragement. After a moment of hesitation, Nicky stepped into Rory's arms and took a seat on the man's lap.

There was a moment of panic when she realized Nicky might recognize Rory from the time they'd spent together. It hadn't taken Maddie more than a second to recognize Rory's voice. What if her son discovered that Santa was only Rory in disguise?

Her fears were quickly put to rest as Rory winked at her over Nicky's shoulder and lowered his voice an octave. "Have you been a good boy this year, spo—uh, son?"

The combination of profound adoration and sober earnestness that graced her son's face brought a lump to Maddie's throat. Her little man had been so brave, had tried so hard. He deserved the best Christmas ever—and then some.

"Yes, sir," Nicky answered gravely, without smiling.

"Ho, ho, ho. Seems to me you've been extra good this year. Now, what can I put on my list to bring you for Christmas?"

"Well, sir," Nicky began hesitantly, then stopped and wriggled his feet.

"What is it?" Rory asked gently.

"I… I'd like to have a model airplane. One of those kinds you glue together? But—" He hesitated and looked imploringly at Maddie.

She smiled her encouragement and nodded for him to continue.

"But what, son?" Rory prompted. His dark eyes brimmed with so much compassion and—*love*—for the boy that Maddie's heart welled until she was sure it would burst.

She held her breath, waiting for Nicky's other request. She hoped that it would be something a little larger than a model airplane. She wanted to go all out this Christmas, grant him his every wish.

"I, um…" Nicky's voice trailed off. He gave Santa a hard, probing stare, which Rory returned with his own strong, clear gaze. The boy pressed his lips together and nodded. "Can you bring my mom something that will make her happy again?"

Maddie heard a buzzing sound in her ears and her head began to spin. Her sight began to fade to tunnel vision. She gripped the armrest of Rory's chair, fighting for control.

Rory placed a warm hand over hers and gave it a gentle squeeze. Immediately, the spots faded and oxygen streamed into her lungs. She turned her hand over and gave Rory's an answering, grateful squeeze.

Nicky licked his lips and swallowed twice, refusing to meet Santa's eyes.

Rory nodded for him to continue. "It's okay," he assured the boy. "You can ask for anything you want. What do you think will make your mom happy?"

"I dunno," Nicky admitted miserably, staring at his swinging feet. "She's like a normal mom in the daytime," he confided, propping himself up next to Rory's ear.

Maddie strained to hear her son's whisper over her rapid heartbeat.

"But sometimes I hear her crying at night. Daddy died, and she doesn't like to talk about it."

Maddie's stomach twisted into a hard knot.

That she was strong enough not to burst into hysterical weeping amazed her. Her poor, suffering son, stifling his own fear and doubts because he had to be the "man" for his mommy.

She barely restrained herself from throwing herself onto Rory's lap and hugging them both. Instead, she stood uncertain, her hands clenched tightly together against the waves of emotion washing through her.

"What is it you are asking for?" Rory questioned softly.

Nicky's eyes lit with enthusiasm as an idea took him. "The Fireman made her laugh. Can you— Yeah! Can you make Mommy fall in love with the Fireman?"

Maddie watched Rory's eyes widen and the corner of his mouth quiver. He must be alarmed by such a request, made doubly potent by the fact that *he* was the man to whom Nicky referred.

Maddie almost smiled despite her own discomfort. Rory was in a pickle if ever she'd seen one. There was no easy out, not even for a man who had made disappearing an art form.

Rory raised his eyebrows at her, his gaze warm and sparkling with mirth. No confusion lurked there—only joy. She felt her cheeks flush under his probing eye.

Rory turned back to the child, his smile fading. "I can't—" He stopped and cleared his throat. "I'm afraid I can't do that, spo—uh, son. Remember, I can only bring things that will fit into my sleigh. I can't make people fall in love."

"But you're Santa Claus!" Nicky protested, bringing a gurgle of laughter to Maddie's throat—despite her distress. "You can do anything!"

"No, son. Not everything. Your mother will have to make her own choice about who to love." Neil wasn't about to let Nicky make the same mistake he'd made as a child. "Have you told God about it?"

"Every night," the boy said with a solemn nod.

"Well, then, that's the best you can do." Neil pressed his lips together tightly, unsure of the storm of emotion in his gut. The little boy and his stubborn, beautiful mother were making his heart ache. He had to consciously remind himself that he was Santa Claus, not Neil March. Santa Claus didn't need a family, what with Mrs. Claus waiting back at the North Pole for him.

Santa couldn't allow Neil March's persistent desire for a wife and son to interfere with what was happening here. He clamped down hard on his jaw, resolute in his determination to play St. Nick to the best of his ability.

"I can't make your mom fall in love," he repeated slowly, "but maybe I can bring her a little something that will make her smile. What do you say to that?"

"Okay," the boy agreed easily. "What?"

Neil laughed, then quickly converted his chuckle to the requisite "Ho, ho, ho." "I'm a little weak in the Mom Department. I was hoping you could think of something."

"I dunno," Nicky said, biting his lip. "Can't you ask Mrs. Claus? She ought to know."

Neil ho, ho, hoed until his stomach hurt. He glanced at Maddie. Her cheeks were a bright pink and her eyes were shining with unshed tears. She looked so vulnerable, and Neil's chest tightened with longing. How he wanted to protect her, to shield her from any more hurt than she'd already experienced.

"I've got an idea," he said, nodding his head toward Maddie. "Mrs. Claus is all the way back at the North Pole. I *could* ask her for advice, but you know what? Your mom is standing right here. Why don't we ask *her* what she wants for Christmas?"

"Good idea," Nicky agreed, looking clearly relieved to have been taken off the hook. "Hey, Mom," he called out. "Come here. Santa needs to talk to you."

Neil let out another genuinely amused "Ho, ho, ho!" and glanced up at Maddie. "Why don't we have Mom come crouch next to us for a picture?" he suggested.

Her soft, moonlight scent wafted toward him as she approached to put her arm around Nicky. Neil smiled and inhaled deeply.

"And what do you want for Christmas, young lady?" he teased, slipping his arm around Maddie and her son.

He knew what *he* wanted for Christmas. A family. He was tired of being alone. He wanted a family to share his dreams with, to laugh and cry with.

And not just any family. He wanted Maddie and her son. To love and take care of and protect. For a lifetime and beyond.

Her smile was syrupy and her big brown eyes blazed as she leaned in toward him. Her breath warmed his ear, and he tightened his grip around her waist in response.

"You've got one coming, you rat!" she whispered from between clenched teeth. "I'm going to get you good for this one. Count on it."

"Oh, I will. I will," he murmured, smiling. Why did the thought of being *got* by Maddie not seem like something he wished to avoid?

To Nicky he winked and nodded. "I think we can handle your mom's request," he said confidently, then finished with a hearty "Ho, ho, ho!"

Nicky beamed so brightly that even Maddie smiled—a moment the photographer-elf caught deftly with a click of her camera.

As quickly as Nicky's smile appeared, it vanished. "If you get something for Mom… I mean, can I still have a model airplane?"

Neil glanced at Maddie, who nodded imperceptibly. "Yes, son, I think I can safely promise you an airplane under the tree on Christmas morning. And if I'm not mistaken, there may be one or two surprises under the tree for you, as well." And one of those surprises would be from him. He hoped Maddie would allow this small gesture, for the boy was coming to mean the world to him.

Maybe he could bring Nicky a puppy. Neil had wanted a dog when he was Nicky's age—a little golden Lab with big feet, floppy ears and a waggly tail. His father had been adamantly opposed to the idea, and, to this day, Neil had never had a pet.

If he were Nicky's father, he'd do things right, showering the boy with all the love and affection he deserved. He made a mental note to ask Maddie about a dog.

Nicky began to crawl off Neil's lap when Neil stilled him with his hand.

"One more thing I think would make a merry Christmas all around," he said, his adrenaline pumping. The idea hit him with such fervor that it made him want to bounce with joy the way Nicky was doing.

He averted his eyes from Maddie for fear she'd read his intention. It was now or never. He wasn't the type to pass by a golden opportunity, especially one so readily presented.

"What?" Nicky and Maddie asked in unison.

"Just this." Without giving her time to think or react, Old Saint Nicholas planted a warm, wet kiss on Maddie's lips.

The elf clicked the camera, capturing the moment for a lifetime of memories.

Chapter Fourteen

❧

"Go long," Celia whispered as Maddie huddled head-to-head with her. "We're gonna finish them boys off completely this time!"

"Break!" mother and daughter shouted in unison.

"Look out, fellas!" Maddie warned as she approached the invisible line of scrimmage. "Gramma's on the rampage. And you both know what that means!"

"Means it's high time we men showed you ladies how to play football," Davis retorted. "Ain't that right, Nicky?"

It was boys against the girls. Nicky and Davis against Maddie and Celia. And the girls were outscoring the boys by a good three touchdowns.

Maddie crinkled her mud-smeared nose at

her step-dad and crouched before the football. "We're gonna wipe you from the face of the earth and you know it!" she taunted playfully.

Nicky set himself to rush, while Davis held back and waggled his eyebrows at Maddie. "Don't count on it, sweetheart. We were just letting you play for a while before we show you what we're really made of."

"Yeah, Mom!" Nicky agreed, his breath coming out in a puff of mist. It was a crisp day, and they were playing in two inches of snow and enough mud to fill a pigsty, but the Colorado sun was brightly shining, its warmth cutting through the chilly air.

They'd all bundled in long johns, followed by jeans and sweatshirts, then snow pants and parkas. It was a wonder any of them could waddle, never mind run with the football, but Maddie was genuinely enjoying herself, and she knew Nicky was enjoying the time with his grandparents.

She was grateful to Davis for suggesting this impromptu game and picnic, though she suspected their picnic would consist of hot chocolate before a roaring fire.

One last down and they'd go back to the house, she decided, gripping the football between her mittened hands. Providing, of course, that she scored a touchdown on this play.

"Are we gonna talk or play?" Celia demanded, glaring cheerfully at the boys. When they growled back at her, she hunched behind Maddie. "Hup! Hup! Hike!"

Maddie tossed the pigskin to her mother and dashed past Nicky and down the length of the park. She continued at a dead run, turning and waving to signal her readiness to receive the touchdown pass.

Davis was hard on her heels, his cheeks red and his breath coming in short, tight gasps. "Gonna get you, sweetheart!"

Maddie ignored him, concentrating on her mother. She played like she meant to live— giving it all she had and enjoying every second.

Just as Celia lofted the ball, Davis sprinted toward her, screaming like a banshee. One eye on the ball and the other on her attacker, Maddie didn't see the half-foot snowbank until it was too late.

She lost her balance and her feet slid out from underneath her. Davis was barreling down on her, looking for all the world like a star linebacker, and going far too fast to stop without colliding into Maddie and sending them both into a rolling pile of arms and legs.

She hoped Davis remembered they were playing *touch* football. The competitive gleam in his eye made her doubt it. She was going to be sore tonight.

Just as she regained her footing, she began to fall backward. The football was high and wide, but within her reach if she dived for it. She had a split-second choice: try to save herself from the crash landing of a lifetime, or go for the ball and take a digger.

Either way, the result would no doubt be a body full of bumps and bruises. Besides, she was playing for keeps.

With a determined shout, she floundered for the ball, reaching for it with the tips of her fingers, willing her arms to extend a little higher. Stretching until she felt her shoulders were nearly popping from their sockets, she clenched the ball between her hands, squeezing it with all her might to keep it from popping out of her grasp. She panted for air and tucked the football hard to her chest so that it wouldn't bounce out when she hit the ground. Which, unless a miracle occurred, she was going to do momentarily.

"I got— Umph!" she shouted as she slammed into something rock-solid, knocking the breath from her with a *whoosh*.

At first she thought the ground was coming up to meet her, that she was falling faster than she anticipated. But the strong arms encircling her waist and the deep chuckle coming from the rock-solid something put that theory to a quick and painless death.

Her pulse elevated even more than the exercise had lifted it. There was only one man whose voice could elicit electric shivers from within her, warming her despite the cold. Rory March.

"Not bad playing for a girl," he whispered. Maddie thrust her elbow into his ribs, but she quickly realized the gesture bruised her elbow far more than it dented his chest.

He shifted, drawing her closer. She froze in his arms. Her emotions were dodging back and forth. She didn't know whether she wanted to kiss him for catching her or punch him in the gut for interfering with her touchdown attempt.

"Thank you, sir," Davis said between huffs of breath. He stopped by Maddie's side and wiped his sleeve across the sweat lining his forehead. "You not only kept my stepdaughter here from taking a nasty fall, but you kept my grandson and me from losing our game to the girls. It's a fine thing you came along when you did. Mighty fine."

Maddie narrowed her eyes and turned on her semi-unwelcome intruder. "I would have scored a touchdown if you hadn't been in my way, you big, meddlesome hunk of muscle. I protest, or call foul play, or whatever it is the referee does when someone cheats!" She tossed Rory a good-natured glare over her shoulder. "Too many *men* on the field."

"It's the Fireman!" Nicky exclaimed, rushing to Rory's side.

"Hello, sport!" Rory greeted, ruffling the boy's hooded head affectionately. "See your mom's been teaching you to play football."

"Yeah, and she's awesome!"

"You've got that one right," Maddie said, trying to wiggle from Rory's embrace. She gripped both hands around his forearm and pushed with all her might, hoping to dislodge his laced fingers and find her freedom.

"Gramma and Gramps are helping me, too,"

Nicky explained. "You should see my gramma pass a football!"

"I did," Rory said, snaking his left arm completely around Maddie's waist and extending his other hand to Celia. "You have a wonderful throwing arm. I'll bet the Broncos are after you to play for them."

Celia primped her hair and giggled like a schoolgirl. With a delighted smile, she placed her hand in Rory's. "Naturally. But I have to turn them down, you know. *Someone* has to stick around and take care of this decrepit old man," she quipped, gesturing toward Davis. "I'm Celia Winthrow, by the way. And this handsome gentleman is my husband, Davis."

It warmed Maddie's heart to see the fond glance that passed between her parents. Her heart gave a sentimental tug, which was quickly squelched when Rory, his arm slung around her shoulder, nuzzled his face into her hair. "You're covered with snow," he whispered against her neck.

And despite her best intentions, she *felt* like snow melting into his embrace even as her mind commanded her to bail out and run for cover. It was bad enough that Rory was openly embracing her, in front of her parents, no less!

But that she was reacting to his nearness absolutely mortified her.

She'd run if she could, but his grip was as strong, and she knew that it was pointless to try to escape.

Celia winked at Maddie, sending her a silent message that she was missing nothing of what was occurring between her daughter and the stranger.

"And this," Celia continued, her voice rising with mirth, "is my grandson, Nicky Carlton. The pretty young woman you're holding in your arms is my daughter, Madelaine Carlton."

Heat flared to Maddie's cheeks, and she stamped her heel down hard on Rory's foot. He didn't even budge, except to bring his mouth down closer to her ear.

"Madelaine." Rory whispered her name with his deep, rich baritone. "It suits you. Strong, but sweet."

Maddie was certain that the red in her cheeks would put a stoplight to shame. Any chill she'd been feeling earlier was long gone, replaced by a dismaying warmth.

"Mom," Maddie said through clenched teeth, "this is Rory March."

"Rory?" Celia repeated, her eyes lighting up with recognition. "Well! How *do* you do?"

Maddie threw her mother a don't-you-even-think-about-it glare and finally wrested herself from Rory's grasp. Or rather, he let her go.

"He was just leaving," Maddie continued without stopping to catch her breath. "I'm sure he's got things to do, places to go, people to see. He owns March's Department Store, you know."

Celia hesitated, catching her daughter's eye with a concerned glance. The inevitable question—the very question Maddie had been trying desperately to avoid since the moment she'd discovered Rory was really Neil March—was thrust silently at her through her mother's gaze.

"Actually, I don't have a single thing to do today," Rory objected happily. "I'd love to join your game. I'm a decent quarterback, too," he added with a grin.

Nicky raced up to Rory, holding out the football. "Can you show me how to catch a long pass, Rory?" he asked hopefully.

"Sure, sport. Go long," he said, pointing to the far end of the park.

"They never grow up, do they?" Celia commented with a chuckle of her own as the men began their scrimmage.

Maddie tossed a look backward, relieved that Rory didn't seem to be following her. She turned her mother toward the end of the park and increased her pace. They walked in silence until she was certain that they were well out of earshot of the men.

"Is Rory related to Neil March?" Celia queried, patting Maddie's hand in a reassuring gesture.

"No," she replied, choking on the word. "Rory *is* Neil March."

"But I thought—"

"I know." She blew out a frustrated breath. "But if you remember correctly, last time we talked, I didn't know Rory's last name. You can imagine how I felt when I found out the truth. I would never have..." She let the sentence trail into silence as they reached a playground.

Maddie seated herself on a swing and began rocking gently. Celia leaned her shoulder against a pole, her white eyebrows furrowed. "Why does he call himself 'Rory'?"

"It's his middle name." Maddie hesitated to offer more, to open herself up to the deluge of questions to which she herself hardly knew the answers.

"You're dating Neil March." Celia was clearly astonished, and Maddie cringed.

How could her mother not be surprised by the revelation? Maddie barely understood it herself. "I'm not *dating* him," she protested weakly.

"But you have feelings for him." It wasn't a question, and Maddie dropped her gaze from her mother's scrutiny.

"I don't know what I feel."

"He clearly knows what *he* feels," she observed with a chuckle.

"What's that supposed to mean?" The question was out of Maddie's mouth before she had time to think, to stop herself from asking.

She braced herself for an answer that she wasn't certain she wished to hear. Whatever inklings her heart held, putting a voice to her suspicions would make them all too real. And far too dangerous.

"It's as clear as the nose on your face," Celia said, looking back at the men, who were sauntering in their direction, passing the football back and forth to Nicky. "You may not be ready to hear it, but that man is in love with you."

Maddie closed her eyes against the waves of emotion washing through her. Rory March was in love with her? But what did she feel for him? How would she ever make sense of the swirling mass of emotions coursing through her?

She'd been considering a relationship with him before she discovered his true identity. When she found out, of course, she thought that she despised him. But that lasted all of two seconds. Until she gazed into those dark eyes of his and got all confused again.

She still couldn't reconcile the fact that her Rory was Neil March, but whatever his name was, she couldn't deny her attraction for him.

And there was no doubt that her mother could see it in her eyes. Celia had always been good at reading her daughter, and Maddie had no reason to believe today would be any different.

She sighed deeply and shrugged in defeat. "I suppose I do have feelings for him. I certainly can't deny I'm attracted to him."

"Physical attraction isn't enough to build a relationship on," Celia commented.

"I know, Mom," Maddie interrupted. "But

cut me some slack here. It's not his looks I'm attracted to."

Celia tittered and clapped a hand over her mouth. Her eyes bubbled with merriment.

"Well, okay, so maybe I've noticed he's the best-looking man on the planet. But really, it's so much more than that." She tilted her head back and watched the clouds forming over the mountains. "Rory is the most gentle, compassionate man I've ever known. He's wonderful with Nicky. And he makes me laugh."

"Sounds serious."

"I'm not going to marry the man," Maddie blurted, her eyes snapping. "Not yet, at any rate. I've still got a lot of baggage clinging to me, some unresolved issues I have to deal with, before I can make any decisions about my future." She dug her boots into the mud under her feet.

"I'm the last person in the world to push you, dear," Celia agreed at once. "I remember just how it feels. Take your time, and enjoy every second of Rory's company. You've caught yourself one good-lookin' fella."

The last sentence was a boisterous exclamation that Maddie knew could travel the short distance to reach the approaching men. "Shh! He'll hear you!" she hissed, appalled.

"Don't care if he does," Celia insisted. "I'm young enough to appreciate a handsome man, and old enough not to care if he knows it."

"*Please* don't embarrass me," Maddie pleaded, not knowing whether to laugh or cry.

Rory approached Maddie from behind and gave her a push, swinging her high into the air. He continued to gently push her as Celia greeted Davis with a kiss.

"I was just telling Maddie that we ought to go back to her house for our picnic. It's getting too cold to be out in this weather much longer. Especially with Nicky. He might catch a chill."

Maddie ignored the fact that Celia had said no such thing. Her mother was quietly protecting her privacy, and Maddie gave her a grateful nod.

As Rory pushed her higher, she threw her head back, letting the wind whip through her hair. The crisp air brushing her face was invigorating, as was the feeling of weightlessness as she rocked back and forth. It had been ages since she'd been swinging. She felt light and free. Laughter bubbled up in her chest.

Rory chuckled. "I doubt anyone's going to

come down with a cold, but I must admit the thought of a warm drink appeals to me."

Maddie opened her mouth to protest, but her mother beat her to it.

"It's settled, then." Celia wrapped an arm around Davis's waist and gave him an affectionate hug. "Now get that girl off the swing and let's go have a picnic."

Neil relaxed into the comfort of a well-used armchair. Closing his eyes, he leaned back, enjoying the sounds of home around him.

Home. That's what Maddie's house felt like. It put his own starkly furnished, utilitarian penthouse apartment to shame.

A steaming cup of marshmallow-laden cocoa warmed against his palm. The aroma of fresh, yeasty bread permeated the air—never mind that it was pizza from the local takeout. Even Max, Maddie's slobbery-jowled bulldog, added to his pleasure, despite the fact that the animal decided to use Neil's foot as a pillow only moments after he sat down, and was at this moment making repulsive snorting noises as he slept.

Neil chuckled and concentrated on more gratifying sounds, such as the fire crackling in the hearth, serving as a background to the cacophony of cheerful voices.

Nicky made loud siren sounds as he pushed his toy trucks across the living-room floor. Celia and Davis stood in the alcove, arguing about the pizza they'd ordered. Celia thought they should have ordered vegetarian for Davis, who was, she reminded him in low, biting tones, on a low-fat diet. Davis, who had eagerly ordered the triple-meat variety, insisted that they were celebrating. And what use was celebrating if he couldn't even cheat on his diet?

Maddie sang lightly in the kitchen. She really did have a lovely soprano. It made him feel warm, content. He counted himself fortunate to be a part of this family gathering.

Maddie had completely ignored his presence since she'd begrudgingly welcomed him, but Celia and Davis were going overboard to make him feel comfortable. He wished Maddie would accept him with the same enthusiasm, but for now it was enough just to be here with her—even if she wasn't speaking a word to him.

He opened his eyes when she entered the living room and warmed herself by the fire.

Rising quietly, he joined her at the mantel. "Thanks for inviting me."

"I didn't invite you. My mother did."

His throat tightened. "Well, thanks for putting up with my presence, then."

"It's the least I could do," she bit out, her voice laced with a sarcasm that stabbed into Neil's gut.

He stuffed his hands into the pockets of his jeans. "Say the word, Maddie, and I'll leave."

He felt her rib cage rise and fall as she sighed deeply. She turned toward him, putting a tentative hand on his chest. "I'm sorry, Rory," she whispered, her voice cracking with emotion. "I don't mean to be so snippy. I don't know what's wrong with me tonight."

He pulled a hand from his jeans and laid his palm against her cheek. "Then let's pretend there *isn't* anything wrong. Just for tonight, Maddie. Can you relax and enjoy the evening? With me?"

Maddie lifted her gaze to him, her wide, brown eyes making his insides shout for joy. Without conscious thought, his other hand moved up to frame her face, to stroke her silky smooth skin with the pads of his thumbs. She was so soft, so vulnerable.

He couldn't help himself. He had to kiss her. Even if she kicked him out the moment he was finished.

He bent his head slowly, waiting for protest, but none came. Maddie closed her eyes and swayed into him, lifting her face toward his.

He brushed his lips across hers, savoring the feel and taste of her. It was all he meant to do. A soft, light kiss, something gentle and benign.

But when she wrapped her arms around his neck and pulled his face closer, he found himself no longer in control of his actions. Moonlight wrapped around him as he deepened the kiss. His heart pounded wildly in his head as she kissed him back.

"Mommy's kissing the Fireman," Nicky calmly informed his grandparents as they entered the room.

"Yes," Davis said, followed by a booming laugh. "We can see that."

"I asked Santa to give him to my mom for Christmas, but Santa said he couldn't do that," Nicky continued in a loud whisper.

"Seems to me maybe they don't need Santa's help," Celia said, patting Nicky on the head. "But I'll be sure to thank him if I happen to see him."

Neil dropped his hands as Maddie jumped away from him, her face flushed. It could be from their proximity to the fire, he supposed, but he hoped *he* was the one causing such an enchanting effect.

Her soft, cinnamon hair was tangled around her cheeks, and her eyes were wide and luminous. It was all he could do not to step forward and wrap her in his arms again.

And if he did, he'd never let go again. He raked his fingers through his hair near the back of his neck, willing himself to back off before he did something irrational. Like drop to one knee and propose.

She wasn't ready for the kind of commitment he desperately needed to give to her. He wanted to marry her, to spend his life trying to make her happy.

But if he proposed, she'd turn him down flat, regardless of how she'd responded to what he'd meant to be a light brush of their lips. He knew without a doubt that her mind was not yet ready to accept what her heart already knew.

She thrust and parried like a professional fencer, withdrawing just when Neil thought she would be advancing on him, and throwing him off every time.

He knew he'd overstepped the boundaries when he'd kissed her, but he also knew she'd wanted that momentary closeness as much as he had. Her response had been genuine, before her mind could override her heart's desire.

But if that were true, maybe his life wasn't doomed to solitary confinement. Maybe he *could* step beyond his past and embrace his future—a future that included Maddie and her son. If he could make her see him as "Rory," the man she believed him to be when they first met… If he could convince her that her response to him wasn't to be feared or thrust away, but embraced and cherished.

If he could convince her that he loved her… everything might turn out right.

"Are you two going to stand there smooching all day, or are we going to eat?" Celia wrapped a hand around Neil's arm and pulled him toward the couch. "Sit here, where you can be with Maddie."

Maddie reluctantly joined him on the sofa and busied herself fixing a plate of pizza for Nicky. Neil watched her for over a minute, but she refused to meet his gaze.

He shifted his glance to Celia and returned her friendly wink with a smile. He knew Maddie felt differently, but he would never be embarrassed by his affection for her, no matter who was watching.

"This evening has turned out far better than I ever expected," Davis said pointedly.

"Thank You, Lord!" Celia exclaimed.

"Amen to that," Neil agreed heartily. He couldn't remember a time when his heart felt so much at peace—not even before the accident. He rested a hand lightly on Maddie's back, but dropped it when she stiffened.

"I know we can't talk here," he whispered into her hair. "But will you meet me tomorrow night?"

She turned to him, her eyes full of questions. But he didn't want questions. He wanted answers—one in particular.

"Maddie, please. Let's settle this between us. Just give me an hour. Say you'll meet me tomorrow night. At eight. At that French restaurant off 16th Street. I'll buy you dinner and we can talk…." His voice dropped off at the end of the sentence.

He was babbling like a teenager asking his dream girl to the prom. Here he was, a man of the world, a man others looked up to and emulated, reduced to feeling awkward and gangly and all thumbs.

Not that it surprised him. Maddie *was* his dream girl; and he could be everything she needed in a husband. All he wanted was a chance to prove it.

She dropped her gaze to her plate. "Excuse me," she said, then bolted from the room.

Neil clenched his jaw. He wanted to follow her, to make her admit she loved him, too.

Maddie tossed her plate on the counter in the kitchen and sat down at the table, swiping a frustrated hand down her face. Her mind raced in circles.

Celia entered with a tentative knock on the door frame. "Is it okay if I join you?" she asked, pulling up a chair without waiting for an answer. "You aren't crying, are you?"

"No, I'm *not* crying," Maddie ground out, slamming her palm down on the table. "But if I were, they would be tears of anger. That man makes me so…"

"So…?" Celia prompted.

"So… I don't know! He makes me feel so many things. Angry. Frustrated. Happy. Loved. Intrigued. Suspicious. Excited."

"And?"

"Loved."

Maddie saw Celia's lips quirk into a smile when Maddie repeated herself, making her feel five years old again, blurting out the truth when she meant to tell a lie. What did love have to do with what she felt for Rory?

"Not a single one of these emotions make any sense to me. They all swirl around together in my brain until I think I'm going to go crazy trying to sort them all out."

"You're not going crazy, dear heart," her mother said, gently, reaching out a hand to squeeze her arm. "It's called falling in love. If we stopped to think about it, not a single one of us would ever do it, because it sure doesn't make a whit of sense."

"It wasn't this way with Peter," Maddie protested. "I didn't feel all giddy and confused."

"You and Peter were both children, dear. You were too young to experience the kind of feelings Rory stirs in you."

"But I did love Peter."

"Of course you did, dear. And a part of you always will. But that doesn't mean you can't embrace what Rory is offering you." Celia paused and took both her daughter's hands.

With a direct, piercing stare, she continued. "I don't know whether you're looking for advice or not, and I know sometimes meddling does more harm than good in affairs of the heart. But, Maddie, that boy is the genuine article. Rory March is one-hundred percent for real."

Maddie was suddenly very conscious of her own breathing. Her mother had the uncanny knack of reading people, and she was almost never wrong. Even considering that they'd only just met. But *could* Rory be "for real"? Could she really hope for a future with him?

And what would she do if she were wrong?

"Give it time, dear. Things always seem to work out when we wait on God."

Maddie nodded, her mother's words calming her.

Celia cleared her throat. "When Davis and I first married, he worked as a carpenter."

"I remember."

"I bought him a wedding ring—an *expensive* ring with diamonds in it. It was probably more than I could afford at the time, and I definitely think I was more than a little obsessed about him wearing it."

She chuckled, and Maddie laughed with her.

Celia's pale gaze clouded as she reached into her past. "Davis refused to wear the ring to work. After your father left, it wasn't easy for me, and I was terrified the same thing would happen with Davis. My fear made me furious, and I lashed out at him."

"What happened?" Maddie asked, squeezing her mother's hand.

"I got over it. Davis was right—that time, anyway."

Maddie chuckled.

"I thought he just wanted to be footloose and fancy-free when he wasn't home. At best, that he didn't want to lose those fancy diamonds. Turned out he was just being plain ol' practical Davis. The man stood to lose a finger doing carpentry with a ring. Could get caught up on the wood or something."

Maddie made a face, and Celia nodded.

"And here I was thinking that he was being vain. Even so, it was hard. Out there in the world among all them pretty women with not so much as a wedding ring for protection. Didn't sound like I had much of a chance to compete."

"But Davis loves you."

"Yes, he does. And that was the very thing I

finally had to get through my thick, stubborn head. A man wearing a wedding ring out the door of his house don't mean diddly. Your father wore one. But wedding rings are notoriously easy to slip off and into a pant pocket."

Maddie's throat tightened. The message was coming through loud and clear.

"Davis isn't your father. And if he's gonna cheat on me, he's gonna do it whether he's wearing a ring or not. But I'm going to make myself miserable if I worry about it."

Celia rose and flashed a smile at her own wedding ring. "I can't control Davis. But I can trust him. The choice is mine. It was my decision then, and it's carried me through to this day."

Celia brushed a hand across Maddie's hair and placed a gentle kiss on her cheek. "That's all I wanted to tell you," she said, and left the kitchen.

Maddie gripped the edge of the table as the hope that had sparked within her fanned to life in her chest, soothing her with its warmth.

She was afraid, as much of herself as of Rory. But fear got her nowhere. Hadn't she learned that from the year she'd hidden from the world?

I can't control Davis. But I can trust him.

Did she have the courage to trust Rory the way her mother trusted Davis?

She wasn't sure. But she was tired of hiding, tired of second-guessing. It was time to move forward, to take the ball and run for the touchdown.

Maddie smiled to herself. Scoring touchdowns was her specialty.

Chapter Fifteen

For the third time, Neil looked at his watch.

She wasn't coming.

He wanted—no, *needed* to tell her what was in his heart. It was time she learned the whole story behind her husband's death. Why the display went up in flames. Where *he* was when it happened.

He prayed for the strength to tell her everything. If she hated him for it, well, he could hardly blame her. For the longest time he'd hated himself. Only now was he beginning to be able to distance himself from it, realize it had been out of his control.

If it came down to it, he would walk away and leave Maddie Carlton in peace, even though it would cost him his heart to do so.

The dynamics between them had changed

on the day he found her in the park playing football. They'd shared something special that night, whether Maddie would accept it or not.

Why wasn't she here? he wondered anxiously.

Because she told him that she wasn't coming. It wasn't as if she'd given him any reason to hope otherwise.

And yet he *had* hoped. She'd been so soft and hesitant when she'd turned him down, as if she weren't sure herself whether it was the right thing to do.

He'd come anyway, an hour early, just in case.

And now she was an hour late.

No, he amended. She wasn't late. She wasn't coming at all. It didn't take a genius to figure that out.

Neil paid his check and walked out into the night air, the darkness closing around him like a cloud. The chill in the air matched the chill in his heart. Downtown Denver would always remind him of Maddie.

He had to let her go. Finally admit she was never really his to begin with, however much he wanted circumstances to be different. He couldn't change who he was: Neil March, her sworn enemy. A few stolen kisses weren't going to change that stone-carved fact.

He paused at the entrance to the Brown Palace Hotel and smiled grimly, pulling his leather jacket more tightly around his chest. He would always remember Maddie as he'd first seen her. Cinderella. Sweet and simple, and all dressed up for the ball.

How her eyes had lit up during the carriage ride, as she exclaimed over the horse and carriage and clapped with joy at the sparkling Christmas lights. How he'd enjoyed her laughter, the brief kiss they'd shared.

Had they met only a few weeks ago? It seemed to Neil like a lifetime. And then some.

In two days it would be Christmas Eve. The mark of the coming of the tiny Baby in the manger who meant life instead of death.

Life.

He needed to face the fact that Maddie Carlton might never capitulate, might never see past Neil March and find Rory inside.

Life without Maddie loomed like a gigantic cavern, empty and echoing. He couldn't do it alone.

But he knew where to go for help.

* * *

In the light of the setting sun, Maddie pulled her small car off the road and into a secluded gravel cul-de-sac. She parked between two eastward-facing cars and turned off the engine. Hers was only one of many cars already parked in what Maddie thought of as "Lovers' Lane."

From the top of the ridge, she watched airplanes take off and land, listening with a heavy heart to the roar of the engines as they passed overhead.

It was a bittersweet reminder, a reunion of sorts. With no money for a *real* date, she and Peter had often sat here watching the airplanes. They'd talked quietly about their hopes and dreams, their future plans, as they watched jets shooting off into the great unknown.

In hushed tones, they had speculated about the people on the plane, and imagined all the exotic places the two of them would someday fly.

They had known even then that there would be clouds, but with the eternal optimism of youth, they never imagined how black and stormy those clouds would be. How the hovering clouds would descend on them, strangling their relationship. And eventually taking Peter away.

It was here, in this car and in this place, that he had proposed to Maddie. If she closed her eyes and put all her effort into it, she could see him still. The way his white-blond hair fell across his forehead and into laughing azure eyes. His contagious, dimpled grin.

He'd been so sure of himself, so confident of her. Of them. She hadn't hesitated a moment in accepting his proposal, believing it to be the most romantic of circumstances despite his not spending a dime on extravagances.

She hesitated now. She'd come here for a purpose, but it wasn't easy to consider, much less perform.

It was time to say goodbye.

She knew that it needed to be said. Aloud. And his grave didn't seem like the right place for such a momentous occasion. The cemetery was a reminder of death. *Peter's* death.

Maddie wanted to remember his life. His laughter. His love.

Peter's spirit was with God. She believed that with her whole heart.

"I believe," Maddie said aloud, "that you loved me. Not only when you proposed, but right down to that last minute, when you walked away from me because you were too angry to talk.

"And I loved you, too. Even when you made me so furious I'd cry. Even when the doubts crept in, making me feel frightened and alone." She paused as a low jet roared over her car. "I loved you with all my heart. I finally recognize that I still love you. I always will. I can accept that now."

She folded her arms over the steering wheel and peered up at the darkening sky. "I don't know what happened to us those last few months. We lost focus…got sidetracked from what was really important.

"But I saw the faith in your eyes the day we made our sacred vows before God and our families. I remember the prayer you said on the eve of our honeymoon, how you asked the Lord to bless and keep us."

She paused to take a deep breath. "I don't know how to work out all of the feelings caught up inside me. We never got to talk. You left too soon. I never knew the truth."

She slammed her palm against the dashboard. "I still don't know. And that's what's eating me up inside. That's what I have to let go of. Not my love for you. Not my past. My *fear*.

"Problem is, I don't know how to do that. If only you hadn't walked away. If only you had told me if—"

She gripped the steering wheel with her fists. "But you never did tell me. We never did talk about it. You went into that stupid display and never came out again."

Leaning her head on her hands, she began to weep. "You abandoned me. You were my husband. You were s-supposed to protect me, take care of me. But instead you left me all alone.

"How am I supposed to raise Nicky? He needs a man around. A father."

She cried until there were no tears left, then rummaged through her purse for a tissue.

"I didn't come here to cry," she said, smiling through her tears. "I came here to tell you that I love you. I love you in spite of your leaving, in spite of whatever differences we had between us. I'm angry. And hurt. But my pain can't bring you back. It can't answer the unanswered questions, and I have to live with that. I have to trust you now like I didn't trust you then. And I have to trust that God knew what He was doing when He left me all alone."

She watched another airplane leave the ground, its methodical, blinking lights reminding her of a heartbeat. "God must have had His reasons for taking you when He did. I can accept that now. And I know—" her voice broke and her heart welled with love and sorrow "—I know you wouldn't want me to go on like I have been. I forgot how to trust. I lost my faith in God and in humankind. And I especially lost my faith in myself."

She smiled through her tears. "I'm ready to move on. I've met someone I want to share the rest of my life with, if he'll have me.

"He won't—he *can't* replace you, Peter. You were my first love. But I think you'd approve of Rory. I truly believe Rory and I are meant to be together, just as you and I were once meant to be together."

Her gentle laughter filled the car. "It feels funny talking to you about this. About another man. I don't even know if you can hear me. But I know God's listening, and I trust Him to relay the message.

"Do you understand?" She allowed the car to fill with peaceful silence. After a moment, she nodded, her chest brimming with love for Peter and Nicky. And for Rory. She had a lot to live for, and without the burden of unanswered questions on her shoulders, the future was bright. "Yes," she whispered into the still air. "I believe you do understand.

"And I think I'm beginning to understand, too." Comprehension suddenly engulfed her. "I thought it was *you* holding me back, and the agony of not knowing the truth."

Peace filled her heart until she thought she might burst from joy. "But it was me all along. It was *my* choice to hate. It was *my* choice to cling to the past.

"It was me all along," she repeated, amazed. "And here I was blaming everyone I could think of except myself—God, you, Neil March. Never accepting the fact that the choice to live—or to waste away hiding inside my shell—is mine."

She watched one last plane ascend to the heights, a smile in her heart. "I've made my choice. I'm going to give life everything I've got. And no matter what, I'm going to be happy."

She took a breath and repeated the affirming statement. "I'm going to be happy, Peter. And I wanted you to know."

Chapter Sixteen

❧

Where was Rory?

Maddie sauntered down the open-air 16th Street mall, glancing behind her every time she detected a movement or a shadow. She was moving beyond irritated into just plain angry.

Two days ago the man had been around every corner, behind every bush. He'd even been Santa Claus, for pity's sake.

But now that Maddie was looking for him, it was as if he had fallen off the face of the planet.

She made a point of being visible, waiting with eager anticipation to see the familiar shadow of her Phantom following her. She ached to tell him the news.

She'd made it right with God. She'd made

it right with Peter. And now she was ready to make it right with her dear, gentle Rory.

Except that she couldn't find the man.

Where *had* he run off to? She'd been grocery shopping, to the dry cleaner's, to the movies, to the mall. All places he'd tailed her in the past two weeks.

She was running out of places to look, and running out of patience.

With a frustrated sigh, she decided to return home. It was Christmas Eve, and the malls would be closing soon, anyway. Walking the mall had been her last-ditch effort to find Rory before Christmas. She had so wanted him to spend the holiday with her and Nicky.

Letting herself in the front door with her key, she inhaled the tangy scent of fresh pine. Silence greeted her. Nicky was at a neighbor's playing, leaving the house unnaturally quiet.

But it wouldn't take much to get in the Christmas spirit. A flip of a switch would get a roaring fire burning in the gas fireplace, and it would take only a few seconds more to tip three tall glasses of eggnog. All she needed to make the cozy scene complete was for her son to return home. And for Rory to materialize out of thin air.

Closing her eyes, she imagined his deep, rich voice as they sang familiar carols together. Or as he told the celebrated story of the first Christmas in hushed, reverent tones while they gathered around the ceramic Nativity scene.

Nicky needed to hear the story of Jesus come to earth to bring peace and goodwill to mankind. Christmas held so many unhappy memories for the boy. It was up to her to bring back the magic.

She needed to remind Nicky of God's constant and enduring love. In her own pain and doubt, she'd let regular church attendance slip into the cracks.

Come to think of it, she could use a little Christmas joy herself. Especially with her spirits so low at not being able to find Rory.

Her house was now fully decorated, with holly and garland strung in every conceivable location. Mistletoe had been added in high-traffic areas, a last-minute touch Maddie was especially pleased with.

If only Rory were here. Mistletoe didn't amount to a hill of beans if there was no one special to share it with.

She peeked out the curtain, hoping to see

his tall, broad-shouldered form leaning on the lamppost across the street. But it was empty.

She could call his office. Or even more daring, she could phone him at home, if he was listed. He'd be home on Christmas Eve. Unless he was with family.

He certainly wasn't with her.

Perhaps he had nieces and nephews to visit. Or maybe he spent Christmas with his parents. She didn't know anything of his family. And suddenly her lack of knowledge seemed like a cavern in her mind, waiting to be filled.

She wanted to know everything about Rory. She'd gathered bits and pieces. How he put hot-pepper sauce on everything he ate. And how children made him smile.

But she ached to know more. Much more.

The sound of the doorbell startled her from her thoughts.

Rory!

She dashed down the stairs and tore open the door, her heart pounding and a gigantic grin creasing her face.

The smile faded when she caught sight of the pale-faced, over-rouged blonde on the other side of the door.

The woman patted her curls, which looked

to Maddie as though they'd been pasted on with superglue. Or at least a decent-size can of hair spray. She had long, acrylic nails and a tall, lithe body that matched her four-inch spiked heels. And she was dressed in so much fur that she looked like a bear with her winter coat on. Not exactly the outfit Maddie would have chosen for appealing for money.

Max waddled to the front door and started woofing, a sound guaranteed to make the most steadfast of mailmen run for their lives. The woman, however, gave Max one quelling glance and stepped a foot backward, not so much from fear of being eaten alive, Maddie thought, as from repulsion over Max's drool.

Maddie sighed. The woman was no doubt representing one charity or another, though they usually weren't so bold as to knock on her front door, never mind face off her dog. Maddie was learning to give from what God— and Rory—had given her, but it was difficult. There were so many good causes. All the money in the world could not end suffering. Only God could do that.

Maddie felt inadequate, especially being face-to-face with the stranger. It was difficult enough to say no to fervent pleas when they were made by telephone or letter.

"I'm Victoria Hamilton," the blonde said, extending her hand.

Maddie shook her hand and attempted to make eye contact, thinking perhaps the obviously nervous woman might be reassured by a friendly smile.

But the woman looked away and clutched her handbag. She shifted from foot to foot, and Maddie had the curious notion she was ready to bolt down the stairs, across the grass and back to the safety of her long, pink luxury sedan. Which would be an interesting feat considering the shoes the woman was wearing. Maddie tried to restrain a smile at the thought.

"Can I help you?" Maddie asked gently, finding herself intrigued by the woman who refused to leave and had yet to say anything more than her name.

"Yes," the woman replied shortly. "No."

Maddie raised her eyebrows.

The woman blew out a breath. "Peter...your husband..." She stopped and wet her glossed lips with the tip of her tongue. "Before he died, the two of us were...meeting together."

Maddie's heart dropped like lead into the pit

of her stomach as all the fear and insecurity she thought she had prayed away came rushing back upon her.

She gripped the doorknob, fighting for control. "You'd better come in," she said grimly, her voice catching.

Mentally, Maddie calmed herself, all the while praying silently for the strength and courage to bear whatever the next few minutes would bring—to face the woman with poise and calm. She didn't have the heart to meet this obstacle head-on, but she *wasn't* alone. And God *was* strong enough.

Maddie seated the woman in her best Queen Anne armchair, then perched on the edge of the sofa. "May I get you something to drink, Ms. Hamilton? Coffee, perhaps?" She was surprised at how calm she sounded, that her voice didn't waver.

"No, thank you, Mrs. Carlton. And please, call me Victoria."

Victoria. Somehow, putting a familiar name to her made the woman all the more real. And all the more daunting.

"And you can call me Maddie," she croaked from a dry throat.

"Maddie." For the first time, the woman met

Maddie's gaze. She had lustrous, almond-shaped emerald eyes. She was a beautiful woman.

Maddie folded her hands on her lap and leaned back, welcoming the firm security of the sofa across her shoulders. She waited silently for the woman to continue. She could see the interplay of emotions crossing Victoria's face, not the least of which were fear and doubt.

The fur-clad woman was in a bizarre and stressful situation, and she had come of her own volition. Perhaps to clear her conscience.

Maddie fought her rebellious anger, mentally replacing it with compassion. And forgiveness. Only in forgiving Peter could she move on with her own life. She could do no less for this woman.

"Maddie, I should have come here a year ago. But I didn't, and I regret that now. I've tried to put it aside, but my conscience will simply not let me be."

Maddie's chest tightened. She had been right. Peter *had* had something going on along the sidelines. She felt a surge of anger, but she ignored it.

She didn't feel right about the events that were unfolding. But she would *do* what was right. For herself. For Nicky. For Peter. For Rory.

And most of all, for God.

"Go on," she said, her voice coarse with emotion.

"I have a story to tell, a story I hope will not distress you too much." She looked Maddie in the eye. "Your husband had a secret."

At least she had the grace to look surprised when Maddie nodded calmly. "Yes. I know."

"You do?"

"Yes. But I'd like to hear it from you. You must have been through a lot to have come to my front door this afternoon."

"Me?" She sounded genuinely surprised. "Well, I guess so. But it's nothing compared to what you've been through. I'm terribly sorry about your loss."

"Thank you," Maddie said in the monotone that was her way of reigning in her emotions.

"It all began about a year before Peter passed away," Victoria started, then stopped and patted her well-starched coiffure.

Maddie could see that the woman was shaking. She should be shaking, coming here like this, she thought.

No. Maddie wouldn't let herself sulk, no matter how badly she hurt inside. Lightly clenching her jaw and hoping Victoria wouldn't notice, Maddie reached for the woman's hands and gave them a reassuring squeeze. "It's okay. You can tell me."

"This is a lot harder than I thought it would be. You can imagine how I agonized over coming here. But you want the story." She dragged in a breath. "You must have noticed how often your husband worked late."

Maddie nodded.

"He didn't want you to know."

Obviously, Maddie thought. Mentally she braced herself for Victoria's next words.

"He wasn't working late, Maddie. At least, not at the accounting firm."

"No?" No, of course not. He felt trapped there, like he had a noose around his neck that tightened with every passing day.

"No." Victoria's gaze pierced her. "He was bundling newspapers."

"He was *what?*" Maddie tried desperately to remain calm, but her outburst still sounded like a shriek.

"Bundling newspapers. Trying to make extra money so he could take you on that cruise you've always wanted."

"Oh!" Maddie felt a tidal wave of relief wash through her, but it was mixed with a healthy dose of guilt for her lack of trust in him. She burst into tears.

Her dear, beloved Peter, secretly working an extra job in order to give *her* the desire of her heart.

Why hadn't he told her? So many arguments could have been instantly stilled, so many doubts quieted.

But he'd wanted it to be a surprise. It was just like Peter. Working so diligently without a word to her. Doing grunge work without a single complaint. Placing an extra burden on his already weighted shoulders. Going above and beyond the call of love. Sacrificing his own pleasure, his own rest, all for her.

If only she had known. If only…

Maddie glanced through tear-blurred eyes at the woman seated across from her, and sobered instantly. Victoria was crying, too, distress apparent on her face.

"I shouldn't have come. I knew there was a risk that I… I've hurt you. I'm so, so sorry for opening old wounds. How you must be feeling!"

"You've *healed* my wounds, Victoria," Maddie said, happiness making her voice bubble.

"My tears are tears of joy. You've reminded me of all the good and special things about my husband. I had no idea he would go to such great lengths for me."

"But I thought you said—"

"I was mistaken. I didn't know. You've—" she choked on the words "—given me a lovely Christmas present. And I have no way to thank you except to express my gratitude from the bottom of my heart."

Victoria rifled through her handbag for a couple of tissues. Handing one to Maddie, she then loudly blew her nose with the other. "There's more," she said hesitantly.

Maddie's heart billowed.

"The cruise. I am—was—Peter's travel agent. He paid for that cruise, but he never set a date." Again, she searched through her handbag, this time retrieving a travel itinerary and some colorful brochures.

"What—?"

"For you. I should have brought them to you a long time ago. But frankly, I was afraid to face a woman who'd just lost her husband to a tragic accident. Especially to hand her two tickets to the honeymoon suite on a cruise line."

"The *honeymoon* suite?" Maddie repeated, astounded.

Victoria nodded. "Peter said the two of you never had a honeymoon."

"That's right."

"He wanted you to have one now. I think it always weighed heavily on his mind that he'd never given you the honeymoon you deserved. He wanted to make it up to you with this cruise."

Maddie stared down at the itinerary in her lap. "And these are…?"

"Some suggestions for your cruise. I thought now that some time had passed, well, that you might be ready to take a cruise." She paused and cleared her throat. "The Caribbean was your dream, didn't Peter say?"

Maddie nodded, her eyes again welling with tears.

"Cruises really are a lot of fun. You can meet new friends. Do lots of sunbathing. Take in all the sights."

Maddie felt her head spinning. It was too much information, too much emotion, too fast. She put up her hands to call a halt to Victoria's rapid chatter. "I don't know about this."

"Of course, it's no problem switching your

accommodations. You don't need to worry about having to stay in the honeymoon suite if you don't want to. I mean…" The color on Victoria's powdered cheeks heightened as she dropped the end of her sentence.

Maddie scrubbed a hand down her face and blew out a breath. She felt more than a little overwhelmed by the barrage of information. She needed time to sort through her emotions. Relief. Joy. Sorrow. Regret.

"I…can't make a decision right now," she said at last.

"Oh, there's no hurry," Victoria rushed to assure her. "I haven't booked a date or anything." She handed Maddie her business card. "You take all the time you want. When you're ready, I'll book you on the cruise of a lifetime."

Victoria stood and made her way down the stairs to the front door, then paused and turned back. "If you decide you'd rather pass, I understand. I can refund you the money. It's no problem."

"I'll think on it," Maddie promised as she waved Victoria off. She had *lots* of thinking to do.

But not now. Just as Victoria exited, Nicky

dashed in from playing at a neighbor's house, and the phone rang.

Maddie quickly tucked the travel brochures into the pocket of her skirt. "Son?" she called as she raced for the phone.

Nicky stopped halfway up the stairs.

"Why don't you go get changed into your church clothes. Since it's Christmas Eve, I thought it might be nice to go to the service at St. John's."

The telephone rang a third time and Maddie blurted the rest of her words in a rush. "I think they're planning to have real sheep and donkeys there—maybe even a camel!" she coaxed.

"Sure, Mom," Nicky agreed with his usual enthusiasm. "A camel? Cool!"

She smiled and waved him off, her heart filled with love and gratitude, as she picked up the phone.

"Merry Christmas!" Maddie announced cheerfully into the receiver.

"It's Christmas Eve," Celia declared without pretense.

"So I've noticed," Maddie replied wryly.

"I called to ask you, Nicky and Rory to drive up to Benton and attend church with us tonight."

"Thanks, Mom, but we're already going to church here." She paused. "Nicky and I are, anyway."

"Rory out of town?"

Maddie sighed. "I wouldn't know. I haven't seen him since that day we played football."

"That's bad."

"No kidding."

"What are you going to do about it?"

Maddie rolled her eyes. Like she hadn't done everything in her power to find the elusive Rory March. "It's getting late, Mom. I've got to go get Nicky ready for church."

Celia mumbled something under her breath. "Okay, then. Have a good night. And, Maddie?"

"Yeah?"

"I'm glad you're going to church anyway."

"Yeah. Me, too."

Maddie gently replaced the receiver in the cradle. Nothing like a concerned mother to make her feel like a child again. But she wasn't a child. She was a stubborn, determined woman who was going to find Rory March if she had to comb every street in downtown Denver for a week.

In the meantime, she wanted to go to church. She needed to say "thank you" for everything she'd learned today, for answers to the questions she'd set aside as unanswerable.

And the Christmas Eve service at St. John's was the perfect place to do it.

Chapter Seventeen

Sheep, goats, a cow, a donkey, several chickens and even a sagging camel gathered round the makeshift crèche. A wide-eyed little girl about Nicky's age clutched her baby doll close to her chest. She was, Neil surmised, supposed to be the Virgin Mary.

Young Joseph—a boy Neil guessed to be a couple of years older than Mary—was clearly and vocally not pleased with the situation. Shifting the cloth tied to his head with a piece of coarse rope, he glared down at the girl, then attempted to snatch the doll from her grasp.

Little Mary wailed, attracting the attention of surrounding adults. Joseph howled and yanked on the doll's hair. "The Baby Jesus is *supposed* to be in the *manger,* stupid!"

"Son!" a young father sternly scolded. "Stupid isn't a nice thing to call someone. Apologize this instant."

"Well, she is," the boy insisted, before crossing his arms and mumbling "sorry" in the general direction of the little girl.

The moment the boy's father turned his back, the boy grabbed the doll's leg and yanked with all his might. The doll's head came loose from its body, and young Joseph waved it in the air, hooting his delight, while Mary burst into fresh tears.

It was a good thing that baby wasn't real, Neil thought with a smile. He patted Joseph on the head, earning him a scowl as the boy wriggled away from him.

The camel, disturbed from his rest, apparently decided he'd had enough of this standing around. One spindly leg at a time, the old dromedary drooped to the floor, heedless of the pair of sheep he nearly squashed in the process.

When the sheep protested, the camel silenced them with a severe hiss, to the delight of the children participating in the crèche.

A man brought two squirming pigs as his offering to the Nativity scene. Children of all ages crowded around, petting the goats, sheep and pigs, crowing in merriment as the animals squawked, bleated and grunted.

Neil wished Nicky were here. With his enthusiasm for animals, the boy would love the display, especially as some of the tamer species were made available for supervised children to pet.

He could just imagine Nicky's eyes shining, his face flushed with delight. Neil felt a lump form in his throat.

He missed Nicky. And he missed Maddie.

A thousand times he had wanted to go back on the promise he made to himself to give her some breathing room, and a thousand times he had forced himself to stay away from anywhere he might meet up with her. He knew beyond a doubt that if he saw her, he'd break his vow.

But he couldn't keep himself from thinking about her, not for one second of one hour. Even when he slept at night, which wasn't very often or very well, Maddie filled his dreams. When he heard a woman laughing, his mind translated it to Maddie's sweet laugh. When he saw a woman with short, cinnamon-brown hair, his pulse would quicken, even when he knew it wasn't her.

He could no more stop himself from loving Maddie than he could stop the sun from shining. Her heart-warming smile and adorable pout had gotten under his skin. On his mind. And in his heart.

He had every intention of finishing what the two of them started the night they met.

He reached out a hand to pet a brown-and-white goat that was nibbling on his pant leg. A new suit, too, Neil mused. Not that it mattered. He could always buy another one.

What he couldn't buy was Maddie's love. Her trust.

His happiness.

When the time was right, he would try to approach her again, though how he would know enough time had passed was a question he couldn't answer. It was ripping him apart inside not to be with her. Touching her. Loving her.

Ironically, it was his love for her that was keeping them apart. She needed space, more time to come to grips with her husband's death. Time to realize that Neil March, the man she hated, and Rory, the man who loved her, were one and the same.

And he loved her enough to give her the

room she needed, hoping beyond hope that when all was reconciled, she would want him by her side and in her life. If she didn't, he didn't know what he'd do.

He moved away from the crowded crèche and into the church. Many people were already seating themselves in the pews, but Neil had somewhere else he wanted to go first.

To the chapel to pray.

Maddie balked when Nicky went straight for the camel, but the boy stopped short when the dromedary hissed and spat at him. A church parking lot, in Maddie's opinion, was not the place for a camel. Especially an ill-tempered one.

"He's sure a grouchy old fellow tonight!" she exclaimed, laying a restraining hand on her son's shoulder. "What do you say we check out the goats?"

Maddie stuffed her hands into the pockets of her parka, wishing she'd brought mittens. It was chilly, and the weather forecasters were predicting snow for Christmas.

Nicky moved from goat to sheep and back, exclaiming his delight when a goat licked his hand. Maddie kept a sharp eye on the ground.

She came from the country and knew what these animals were capable of.

She experienced a moment's regret that Nicky hadn't had the advantage of country living. He certainly enjoyed animals, and the fresh country air would do him good. Maybe she should consider moving....

She shook her head. She couldn't consider anything until she'd spoken with Rory.

"Hey, Mom, look! A pig!" Nicky exclaimed, pushing a black-and-white potbellied pig by its haunches toward her.

A *pig?* Who put a pig in the Nativity scene? Granted, it made a great addition to the petting zoo, but she couldn't remember ever having heard of pigs being present at the holy birth. Then again, maybe they were. In any case, Nicky was having a blast.

She glanced at her watch. "Only a couple more minutes, son, then we'll have to head inside." She looked to see if Nicky had heard, but his attention had been drawn elsewhere.

His blue eyes, so like Peter's, were huge and brilliantly aglow in the setting sun. And they were locked on the manger underneath the awning where a young Mary and Joseph were kneeling.

"Look, Mom. It's Baby Jesus." He started to walk toward the scene, then stumbled and stopped. He looked back at Maddie, his gaze uncertain. "Is it okay if I…"

"I'm sure it is, son. I'm right behind you."

Reassured by his mother's answer, Nicky approached the awning, his eyes and smile widening as he looked down into the manger. His mouth formed a perfect O as he stared in wonder.

Maddie gaped, too, as she approached the crèche. Of all the incredible notions! Someone had placed a serene, plump-faced sleeping baby boy in the cradle of hay. A very *real* baby boy.

The way Mary and Joseph were carrying on, arguing over whose turn it was to kneel before the child, it was a wonder the poor baby could sleep. The older children's parents soon shushed them as the sun finally dropped underneath the outline of the mountain peaks majestically rising in the distance.

With more people arriving as the time for the service drew near, the area around the Nativity became crowded. Maddie waved her arms at Nicky, hoping to pull him away so they could find a decent pew.

But Nicky didn't notice his mother's gestures. His eyes were locked on the sleeping baby.

Maddie held her breath as the boy reached out a tentative hand to stroke the baby's pink cheek. When he glanced back at Maddie, his eyes were misty with unshed tears.

"Can I...give him something?"

Maddie gulped down her initial reaction, an immediate refusal, when she saw the earnestness in his eyes. He had to know that the baby sleeping in the manger wasn't the real Baby Jesus. She'd discussed it with him before they came. What he would see. What they would do.

She was certain he hadn't misunderstood. She'd been clear that these events had happened many years ago. She'd answered the dozens of questions he pelted her with as best she could. Who, after all, really knew why God had chosen to come to earth as a tiny infant with nowhere to sleep but a manger? And had He really slept on hay?

Maddie didn't even know if pigs had been present.

Unable to speak, she nodded her assent.

With a double-dimple smile, Nicky turned back to the baby. Slowly, reverently, he removed his favorite superhero watch from his wrist. He looked at it long and hard, his fist tightening around the band. Then he took a deep breath and gently laid the watch beside the sleeping infant.

When he turned back, his cheeks were flushed with pleasure and his eyes were filled with love.

"Unless you change and become like little children, you will never enter the kingdom of heaven."

In that moment, Maddie understood. Nicky gave a gift to the representative Baby Jesus for the same reason adults kept up the facade of Santa Claus long after they finally realized that reindeer didn't fly.

Because underneath it all, deep down in the heart of every person, was a still, small voice declaring that love is real.

Maddie walked beside her silent son as they entered the sanctuary and found seats at the end of a row near the middle of the church. Not so far back that they would be unable to see and hear well, but with easy access to the aisle should Nicky need to use the bathroom.

She put her hand into her skirt pocket, smiling to herself when her fingers closed around the travel brochures. It was a lovely gift, even if it would never be used. Maddie knew she wouldn't be able to use those cruise tickets—not without Peter.

Somehow, though, love transcended all that. It beamed through the murky waters of life like a spotlight. She could enjoy her love for Peter, her thankfulness for their time together, and still move forward with her life. She had love overflowing, plenty to go around. For Peter, Nicky, and even Rory, if he wanted her.

Love was, is and ever shall be. That was the way God made it. And love was the reason she could embrace the past, enjoy the present and hope for the future.

As the organ began filling the cathedral with the rich tones of "Joy to the World," Maddie slipped an arm around her son and opened her hymnal.

Her heart swelled with love. She felt like singing.

Chapter Eighteen

Neil paused after praying to light a candle in remembrance of Peter. He ran a hand down the side of his face, his fingers finding the soft, puckered skin of the scar that marred his temple.

For the first time since that Christmas display had turned into a deathly inferno, Neil felt no guilt, and only a mild sense of regret. His soul was clean. God had long ago forgiven him for his part in the accident. But only now had he finally learned to forgive himself.

He still felt restless, but he couldn't place it. Some unnamed anxiety fluttered in the back of his mind, and he resolved to put it aside, at least until the service was over.

He could hear the strains of "Joy to the World" through the thick chapel door, and wondered if it would cause a commotion for him to slip out into the main sanctuary.

Of course, the chapel *had* to be located in the middle of the right wall, rather than at the back of the church, where he would have been able to make a quiet exit.

He chuckled. He was making a mountain out of a molehill. Besides, he was missing his favorite hymn. All he had to do was slip through the door and into the nearest pew. Such a trivial action would hardly hold up the service.

He gripped the handle and slowly pulled the door back, praying it wouldn't squeak. He breathed a sigh of relief as the door closed behind him, but it was short-lived.

"Look, Mom! It's the Fireman!"

At the familiar sound of Nicky's voice, Neil froze. His peaceful smile faded as his restlessness turned into full-fledged churning.

His gaze met that of the woman he wanted most in the world to see, and had tried hardest to avoid.

His heart hammered in his chest during the long seconds he stood motionless, his brain whirling with the options available to him. He couldn't possibly walk past Maddie without a word. She and Nicky had both seen him.

More to the point, he didn't want to walk away. He wanted to sit down in the pew between them and put his arms around them both.

He shrugged off a sense of foreboding and threw caution to the wind. He'd break his vow and spend time in their company. Just a minute or two. Such a minor concession couldn't hurt. They were in church, after all. And he *hadn't* followed her here.

He nodded his head in greeting, expecting Maddie's eyes to flare with anger and mistrust, emotions that would help Neil keep his distance, make it easier for him to excuse himself and break away.

Instead, he found her huge brown eyes warm, inviting. He even thought he saw a flicker of something more.

He was imagining things. He must be. But when she extended her hand toward him, he covered it with his own.

"Rory. I mean, *Neil*. It's nice to see you."

Whatever he'd expected to hear from her mouth, that wasn't it. A few days ago she'd gone to great lengths to get rid of him. She hadn't shown up when he'd invited her to dinner. And now she was welcoming him like an old friend, though he hoped all her friends' hearts didn't lurch like his was doing. He swallowed hard.

"You don't have to…call me Neil," he said hoarsely, feeling as if he were strangling. "I've always…thought of myself as Rory with you."

Maddie nodded. "Rory." Her tongue rolled over the syllables, savoring them like a chocolate truffle. Her eyes affirmed his words. He was "Rory" to her.

There was no condemnation, no distrust.

This is it, his mind confirmed, and his heart soared. Here, in church, was the opportunity he had prayed for. He could make everything right again.

It was time to tell all, and take the consequences, come what may. He loved this woman with the boy. He needed with all his heart to claim his place by her side.

"Mind if I share your hymnal?" he whispered, ruffling Nicky's hair.

Surprise crossed Maddie's features, but only for a moment. She bent down and whispered to Nicky, who scampered to the other side of her, leaving a spot free for Neil.

He stepped in next to her, inhaling her sweet, moonlight scent. Her hand felt warm where their fingers met holding the hymnal.

She was trembling. And he wanted to hold her and comfort her. Desperately.

And if it weren't for the hundreds of people lining the cathedral pews, he would.

"What are you smiling about?" Maddie whispered, seeing the corner of his lips quirk. She elbowed him lightly in the ribs when his shoulders began to shake.

"Tell you later," he whispered back. "That's a promise."

Later.

With amazing swiftness, Maddie's holiday spirit when from glum to exhilarated. Could it be that she would not be spending Christmas alone? Or was she reading too much into a single smile?

Eggnog, a blazing fire, mistletoe—and Rory. It was a scene that warmed her heart.

She closed her eyes to listen as Rory began to sing. The congregation had moved on to "Angels We Have Heard on High," a song that suited his rich baritone to perfection.

She could stand here all night singing Christmas carols, blending her soft soprano with his deep tones, inhaling his spicy male scent. And when he covered her hand with his own and their fingers entwined, it felt like the most natural thing in the world.

Reality intruded like an alarm clock on an early morning when Nicky shifted on his feet and yanked at her sleeve. "I don't know this one, Mom!"

Maddie put a finger to her lips, silently reminding her son not to talk in the middle of a church service.

Rory leaned around Maddie and gestured to Nicky. "Why don't you come stand next to me, sport? That way you can holler if I sing off-key."

Nicky beamed and launched himself at Rory, who, caught off guard, nearly tossed the hymnal in favor of the boy. Both of them broke into muffled laughter, which Maddie chilled with a warning look.

Rory pulled a face and shrugged.

And she thought six-year-olds were trouble!

Smiling at the gentle lapping of peace washing through her, she attempted to shift her thoughts to the service. Her heart stood amazed at how easily Rory fit into their lives. As if he belonged here. As if it were meant to be.

She was intensely aware of how the three of them sat, Nicky sandwiched snugly between the two adults, Rory with his arm casually slung around the back of the pew, his fingers lightly dusting her shoulder. They looked for all the world like a family.

And Maddie felt safe. Warm. Wonderful. Loved.

Chapter Nineteen

Even Nicky forgot to squirm as the revered tale of the first Christmas was told, and when the lights were dimmed for the final Christmas hymn.

Only the cross at the front of the sanctuary remained illuminated as the acolytes passed their vibrant flame from row to row, candle to candle, down the aisles.

"Hold the candle steady," Maddie whispered in Nicky's ear. "Don't touch the flame."

She was more than a little anxious about allowing her young son to have a candle of his own, but his eyes had been so bright when he'd asked. She couldn't refuse him.

But as Rory bent to light Nicky's candle with his, she saw the boy's expression turn from delight to sheer terror. Too late, she realized the threat the fire represented: the nightmare her son would never be able to forget.

To Nicky, fire was the ultimate enemy. It was bad. It had torn his daddy away from him. It had left scars, both internal and external. It was something to be feared.

It's okay, Nicky. You don't have to light your candle if you don't want to. The words were on the tip of her tongue, clamoring from the depths of her soul.

But Rory was already kneeling by the boy, laying a strong, comforting hand on the boy's shoulder.

"It's okay," Rory soothed, and Maddie felt the tension drain from her shoulders. Rory was here. He would say the words.

But he didn't. He just looked deep into Nicky's eyes, slowed the child's breathing by matching it with his own.

"Look at the flame, Nicky," Rory urged, slowly moving his candle between them. "Do you trust me?"

Nicky's eyes widened, but after a moment's hesitation he nodded.

"This fire won't hurt you." Rory's voice was deep and even, his gaze steadily locked with the boy's.

Maddie held her breath, wanting to stop Rory from pushing Nicky too fast. Her brain felt frozen, her tongue unable to form the words.

"You see, Nicky? You can hold this fire. Do you want to hold it?"

No! Maddie's mind screamed, but her mouth remained rebelliously quiet. Why was Rory pushing Nicky so hard? He was just a boy!

Nicky reached out a tentative hand. Rory wrapped it around the candle, keeping his own hand on top of the boy's until he stopped shaking.

As Nicky stood staring at the flame in his hands, Rory stood and lit Maddie's candle.

Maddie didn't know whether to laugh or cry. But when she met Rory's eyes she read there understanding, not only of her fear, but of the boy's.

She glanced back down at Nicky, who was still quietly staring at his candle. Holding the fire, containing it, controlling it, was exactly what he needed to do.

And Rory had known.

Nicky's eyes were still wide with fear as he held the tiny flame aloft, but his fear was mixed with pride.

The sanctuary glowed with the luminescence of hundreds of candles as the congregation began singing "Silent Night" a cappella.

It was the one hymn to which Nicky knew all four verses. Still carefully holding the candle in two fists, he sang the carol with all the joy and reverence of childhood. If he sang a little off-key, no one noticed. The choir of voices echoing through the cathedral sounded almost heavenly.

Rory moved to her side and put a gentle arm around her shoulders. She looked up into his face and saw in his eyes the reflection of the flame.

He smiled.

She returned the smile and leaned into the strength of his muscular frame. Together, they finished the hymn, Rory's magnificent baritone blending with Maddie's hesitant soprano. And Nicky, with his high, squeaky little-boy voice, made the trio complete.

When the hymn was over, the lights remained low. People blew out their candles and spoke in hushed voices as they bundled up in their winter wear and made their way toward the back of the sanctuary.

Maddie's heart began beating in her throat.

Everything had been fine as long as the service had been going, and when she and Rory could be together without tension, without the pressure of making conversation.

He had said they'd talk later. But he really had no reason to stay, other than to tell her what he'd been smiling at earlier. It didn't seem like much. And she *had* to make him stay.

Her mind scrambled for something to say, something benign that would keep Rory by her side while she figured out what to do.

He was clearly lingering, leaning his hip against the edge of the pew, arms folded across his chest as he watched her flutter around, digging through her purse, helping Nicky into his jacket.

She didn't know what to do with her hands. And she didn't want to look at Rory. She had been so anxious to see him, to tell him of her love, proclaim it from the highest mountaintops. It had appeared incredibly easy, in her mind.

But now that he was here, she found herself tongue-tied and visibly shaking. The butterflies in her stomach were doing loop-de-loops. Some had even escaped to whirl around in her head.

What in the world should she say? And what

would she do if he turned around and left before she said anything?

Stop! Wait! You can't go yet. I love you!

"Yeah, right, Maddie. Classy," she mumbled to herself.

"Mom?" Nicky asked, pulling on her elbow.

She glanced down to find her son had been joined by several of his Sunday-school friends. She smiled and nodded at each boy.

"They're serving cookies and hot cocoa in the fellowship hall," Nicky explained, his gaze brimming with excitement. "Can I go down with my friends?"

Maddie smiled. Nicky never had been one to resist a cookie. "Sure, son. But don't you boys make a ruckus," she warned.

"We won't," the boys said in chorus, racing for the back of the sanctuary.

Chuckling at their laughter, she met his gentle gaze. He brushed his hand through the hair near her cheek, then stroked her chin with the back of his fingers. "Well," he said after a full minute of simply staring into her eyes, "guess we've got a few minutes to ourselves. And we *do* need to talk."

Maddie nodded. "Yes. We do." It was difficult to pull herself from the magnetism of

Rory's gaze. She could easily lose herself in those dark, flaming eyes. She mentally fortified her bulwarks, knowing that the time had come to put things right.

And there was no guarantee as to what that would mean to her future. She shivered in apprehension.

Facing one another, they sat down together in the nearest pew. Rory gently touched her shoulder, then his hand dropped away.

"It's time that we—" she began.

"You need to know—" he said at the same time.

He chuckled. His low, rich voice sent shivers tingling down Maddie's spine. How she loved this man! And how afraid she was to admit it.

"Ladies first." He nodded for her to continue.

"No, you first," Maddie insisted, her heart in her throat. She had to blurt out the truth before she lost the ability to speak completely.

"I love you," they said in unison.

Maddie broke into nervous laughter, which was echoed by Rory's deep chuckle.

"You do?" she asked, tears of relief and joy pooling in her eyes.

Rory cupped her chin in his palm and met

her eyes. She could see the truth there, the warmth of love radiating from those obsidian depths. "You bet I do, lady. I think you stole my heart the night you appeared in my life as Cinderella."

"And you, my mysterious Phantom." She placed her hand over his. "I've got so many things I want to tell you."

His eyes clouded and his smile washed away as if it had never been. Maddie questioned this sudden withdrawal with her gaze, but he looked away.

"What is it?" she whispered, her voice rough with emotion. She couldn't imagine what had brought about the sudden change, but a definite chill had filled her heart as the gap widened between them.

"Maddie, I..."

She turned his hand over and laced her fingers through his. His hand felt so warm and strong, enveloping hers. "There is nothing you can say that will change my love for you, Rory March."

"No?" His eyes blazed. "What about the fire that took Peter's life? I'm responsible for that, and you know it."

"I do know," Maddie agreed quietly. "I know

that, in my helplessness—and grief—I turned my anger on a name. Neil March. A faceless man I could make any sort of despicable creature my mind cared to create."

With her free hand, she stroked a finger down his strong jawbone, then turned his head so she could meet his eyes. "Neil March gave me an outlet for my rage, a way for me to feel in control. A place to lay the blame."

"Yes, but I *am* Neil March," Rory protested, his voice lowering an octave.

She felt his grip tighten on her fingers. "No, Rory. You're not the man I imagined. The Neil March I created doesn't exist. You..." She shook her head, smiling gently. Her heart felt ready to burst, she was so happy. The man she loved returned her affection!

Yet she could see the self-condemnation, the loathing in his eyes. All the times she'd reamed Neil March, not knowing she was talking to the man himself, rose to haunt her, and she wished them away. Her mind searched for something to say, something to bring him into her arms, not only now, but forever.

"You feel responsible. I understand that. It was your store. But it was an *accident,* Rory.

The police investigated and cleared your store of any blame."

A sound came from Rory's chest that was a cross between a groan and a snort. "Of course they did. Money talks, Maddie. And walks. And clears the guilty in the public eye. But I was there."

Maddie's throat tightened. "What do you mean?" she asked, her mouth dry. Her stomach spun as madly as her thoughts. She was on a precipice, and Rory's next words would either sweep her off her feet and into his arms or over the edge and into the darkness.

Rory's gaze pierced hers. "I mean, I was *there* that day. The day of the fire." He ran his hand over the scar.

"I never... I mean I..." Maddie tried to speak, but words left her as the scene of the fire flashed into her mind. Peter and Nicky entering the workshop display. The cottony snow bursting into a fiery inferno. A man carrying Nicky out of the flames.

Look, Mom! It's the Fireman!

Understanding hit Maddie as the details came together. The mad whirling in her chest was an almost physical sensation.

Rory was the man who saved Nicky's life.

"It was you." She leaned forward, touched the soft, puckered scar with her fingertips. "Nicky knew. He's known all along it was you."

Rory nodded and swallowed twice in rapid succession. "I wanted to save Peter, Maddie. I tried." He clenched his hands into fists as his face contorted with pain and frustration.

"I know." And she did. It was clear as the dawn of a new day. The man she'd blamed as the culprit was actually the hero. She'd spent months hating the man who had rescued her son.

Rory's tortured eyes met hers. "When I jumped through the flames into the workshop, Peter was struggling with Nicky. He thrust the boy into my arms, begged me to save him. I—" he drew a ragged breath "—I promised Peter I'd be back. I *promised*."

"What happened?" She could see each moment of the excruciatingly painful scene in her mind. Only this time, the soot-covered face of Nicky's rescuer was Rory's.

A shirtless, soot-covered man stumbled from the inferno, a small, drooping form in his arms.
"Nicky!" Maddie choked out the name.

Paramedics swept the boy from the man's arms just as Maddie rushed forward.

Oh, God, no! Her soul cried out to heaven as she approached the still, charcoal-dusted form of her son.

They were wrapping him in sterile bandages, gently coaxing an oxygen mask over his nose and mouth.

"Is he...?" Maddie stammered, touching the shoulder of a waiting paramedic. "I'm his mother."

"He's alive," the man said crisply.

Maddie's shoulders slumped in relief.

"But we're taking him to Children's Hospital. You can ride with him if you like." The man turned a grave face toward her. "He's been burned pretty badly, ma'am."

Maddie's breath caught in her throat. "Will he...?" she began again.

The paramedic's eyes clouded with compassion as he shook his head. "You'll have to wait until we get to the hospital."

"Of course," Maddie agreed dully, her voice nothing more than a squeak.

But what about Peter? He was still inside the blaze. How could she go with Nicky when Peter had yet to be rescued?

Her mind pulled for an answer while her heart pumped furiously.

Just as suddenly, she was enveloped with calm, and she reached for it, embraced it. She knew what to do.

Peter would want her to go with their son.

She turned toward the ambulance.

"Let me go!" *The man's voice was low and threatening.*

The sudden commotion momentarily distracted Maddie. She glanced over to see the soot-covered man who had rescued her son struggling between two uniformed firemen, who were holding him by his arms.

"Let me go!" *the man demanded again, his voice coarse from smoke. He wrenched this way and that, clearly trying to wrestle from their grasp.*

All Maddie could make out of the man was his broad shoulders and coal-black hair. Or was that soot?

But when he turned his face toward her, she gasped in shock. One whole side of his face had been burned.

"I've got to go back in there!" *the man insisted, seemingly unaware of his injury.*

"You've been burned," *one of the firemen*

reasoned, keeping his voice at a low, even timbre. "We're taking you to the hospital."

"No!" the man yelled, loud enough—despite the crowd—for the sound to echo off the walls. "I must go back! There's still a man in there!"

The firemen continued to restrain him.

As the ceiling of the workshop collapsed, there was a rushing sound and a billow of flame.

"No-o-o-o!" the soot-covered rescuer screamed, echoing the agony of her own heart.

"Peter!" Maddie cried simultaneously, reaching her arms out in a powerless gesture.

"P-e-e-e-t-e-r-r-r!"

"Maddie?" Rory took her by the shoulders, his voice low and gentle.

"They wouldn't let you go back for him." It was barely more than a choked whisper.

Rory's shoulders slumped as he recalled the event that haunted him with such ferocity. He'd given his *word*. But the firemen were too strong for him. He'd tried. God knew he'd tried. But they forced him into the ambulance, literally manhandling him despite his adamant protests.

And then it was too late. The workshop made

a nightmarish *whooshing* sound as flames engulfed it. A man was dead, and Neil was helpless to stop it.

"When I found out Peter died in that fire, I lost faith. I had been so sure of myself, so ready to conquer the world single-handedly. Even when the fire broke out, I still thought I was in control. But I wasn't."

He paused and swiped a hand down his face. "It's taken me a while to realize I never *have* been in control. I'm not even supposed to be. It was God all along. I placed my faith in the wrong person."

Maddie reached for his hand and gave it a reassuring squeeze.

"I should have learned my lesson. Trusted God. But I couldn't. My father let me down, and then I let myself down. I thought God would do the same."

"God isn't like that," Maddie said, "though I'm a fine one to talk about great faith and trusting God."

"You're wonderful." He hugged her to his chest, filling the empty ache inside with Maddie's love. "I thought God was punishing me when I met you."

"Gee, thanks."

Neil chuckled. "That came out wrong, didn't it? What I meant to say is that I felt it was divine retribution of some sort to fall in love with the one woman who could never love me back. And all because Peter died in my store, and ultimately, I was responsible."

"I love you, Rory March." She squeezed his ribs, making him feel like a giant teddy bear.

He liked it.

"Peter is with God. And you're here with me. Let it go. God forgave you. I forgive you. All that's left is for you to forgive yourself."

He chuckled again, and this time the laughter reached his heart. The restlessness he'd earlier experienced was replaced by a warm glow that felt to Neil like a crackling hearth on a cold winter's night.

"I was so blind." He pulled back, framing her face with his hands, laughter and love welling in his chest. "He wasn't punishing me when He put you in my life. He was giving me the greatest gifts I could ever imagine. He sent his Son." He nodded to the ceramic Nativity scene at the front of the church, shadowed by the cross above it. "And then he sent *you,* Maddie. You and Nicky."

Maddie launched herself into his arms. He

spun her around with a whoop, then planted her firmly on her feet again, his voice echoing in the empty sanctuary.

"Your love is all I've ever wanted, more than I ever hoped for. I love you. And I want to spend every day of the rest of my life proving that to you. Will you marry me, Maddie?"

She nodded, tears pooling in her big brown eyes. Smiling, Neil dabbed at the wetness on her cheek with the pad of his thumb.

"I'll ask Nicky, too. Man to man. I want this to be as easy on him as I can make it. I love him too much to hurt him."

"He *did* ask God to make me fall in love with you, remember?"

"So he did." Neil hesitated, then broached a tender subject. "Um, speaking of Nicky...?"

Maddie raised an expectant eyebrow.

"I hoped, I mean I thought that if we spent Christmas together..."

"Yes?"

"I bought Nicky a gift."

"Rory, that's so sweet!"

"I'm not so sure you'll say that when you hear what I got him."

Maddie laughed. "Surprise me."

"Can't do that. This is the kind of gift a mother needs to be prepared for."

"Please don't tell me you bought him a car. He's only six, Rory."

Neil laughed. "No car. I, um…bought him a puppy."

"A *what?*"

"A dog." Neil held up his hands to suspend her protest. "He's a yellow Lab, top-of-the-line champion."

"We have a dog. Max, remember?"

"How could I not? He drooled on my feet." He chuckled. "I wanted to get Nicky a dog of his own, something of the non-drool variety."

"Oh, Rory, that's so sweet!" she exclaimed, bussing him on the cheek.

"It is?" he asked, expecting further argument.

"Nicky's been asking for a dog of his own for ages. He'll be so thrilled!" She wrapped both arms around him and squeezed until his ribs hurt.

"All right, already. Enough gratitude. Now, weren't we talking about a wedding? I want a big one, but I want it soon."

"Then we need to enlist Mom's aid. She's

a wonder at pulling big productions together fast."

"Then we'll get ahold of Mom first thing Monday morning," he agreed easily, his business acumen momentarily clicking into gear. "And I'm sure Davis will want to help, too. But first—" he wrapped his arms around Maddie's waist and leaned down until their foreheads were touching "—we have one other small item of business to take care of."

"We do?"

"We do. I promised to tell you what I was chuckling about earlier. I was..." He brought his face closer to hers. He could feel the warmth of her sweet breath against his lips, and his pulse doubled. "...going to kiss you."

"In church?" Maddie whispered with a shaky smile.

"Can you think of a better place to seal our love?"

"I must say I'm relieved that you at least waited till the sanctuary cleared."

"It was difficult, believe me."

"I can't believe you were thinking about such things in the middle of the church service! You were supposed to be paying attention to the service and—"

"Maddie," Neil murmured over her lips.

"Mmm?"

"Shut up and kiss me."

Maddie willingly complied.

Epilogue

Maddie gripped her cream-colored satin wedding dress in one fist and the sleeve of Davis's tuxedo in the other. At the far end of the church, Rory was waiting, but there was a lot of space and a sea of faces on her way to his side.

"Nervous?" Davis asked with a low chuckle.

"No," Maddie growled through clenched teeth. "Mom put a stupid penny in my shoe for good luck, and it's killing me."

"Can you walk with the weight on your heels?"

"Not a chance, with these spikes. What possessed me to have a big church wedding, anyway?"

"You didn't have one the first time around, since you and Peter eloped. Besides, you're a fancy society lady now. Both the major news-papers are covering this event."

Maddie rolled her eyes as her stomach flut-tered. "Don't remind me." She *was* nervous, despite what she told Davis. She didn't have a single qualm about tying her life to Rory's, but she definitely feared making a spectacle of herself in front of three hundred people and the five-o'clock evening news.

The wedding march started and Davis pat-ted her hand. "Time to go. You ready?"

"Yeah. Just don't walk too fast or I'll roll down the aisle instead of floating gracefully like I'm supposed to do."

"Don't worry," Davis assured her. "I'm not going to mess up my only chance to walk my daughter down the aisle."

Maddie tightened her grip on his arm and they began their slow march toward the front of the cathedral. Happy faces rose before her. Aunts and uncles she hadn't seen in years. Good friends from the local university, where she'd just begun taking classes in occupational speech therapy. And her mother in the front row, dabbing at her tears with her tissue.

Maddie's eyes widened as she realized Celia was holding Nicky's squirming yellow Lab puppy in her other hand. Who had let a dog in church?

Panic seized her. Something was going to go wrong. *Everything* was going to go wrong. And then there would be no honeymoon at the Brown Palace Hotel.

Then she looked forward, meeting Rory's loving gaze with her own. Nicky stood proudly beside Rory, her "little man" the best man for the day.

Her eyes shifted back to Rory, who held out his hand to her. Love shone from his face, calming the turmoil inside her. The crowded cathedral vanished as she stepped forward, and Rory's warm hand enveloped hers.

He smiled down at her, mouthing "You're beautiful" before turning her toward the minister. Her heart melted as he repeated the vows in his rich, deep voice—vows she echoed loudly, clearly, for the world to hear.

She was facing her future, her love, her life, and she wanted everyone to know. Finally, the minister declared the groom could kiss the bride, but Rory was a tad too slow.

The bride kissed the groom.

* * * * *

LARGER-PRINT BOOKS!

GET 2 FREE
LARGER-PRINT NOVELS
PLUS 2 FREE
MYSTERY GIFTS

Love Inspired®

Larger-print novels are now available...

LARGER-PRINT BOOKS!

GET 2 FREE
LARGER-PRINT NOVELS
PLUS 2 FREE
MYSTERY GIFTS

Love Inspired®

SUSPENSE
RIVETING INSPIRATIONAL ROMANCE

Larger-print novels are now available...

YES! Please send me 2 FREE LARGER-PRINT Love Inspired® Suspense novels and my 2 FREE mystery gifts (gifts are worth about $10). After receiving them, if I don't wish to receive any more books, I can return the shipping statement marked "cancel." If I don't cancel, I will receive 4 brand-new novels every month and be billed just $5.49 per book in the U.S. or $5.99 per book in Canada. That's a savings of at least 19% off the cover price. It's quite a bargain! Shipping and handling is just 50¢ per book in the U.S. and 75¢ per book in Canada.* I understand that accepting the 2 free books and gifts places me under no obligation to buy anything. I can always return a shipment and cancel at any time. Even if I never buy another book, the two free books and gifts are mine to keep forever.

110/310 IDN GH6P

Name _____ (PLEASE PRINT) _____

Address _____ Apt. # _____

City _____ State/Prov. _____ Zip/Postal Code _____

Signature (if under 18, a parent or guardian must sign) _____

Mail to the **Reader Service:**
IN U.S.A.: P.O. Box 1867, Buffalo, NY 14240-1867
IN CANADA: P.O. Box 609, Fort Erie, Ontario L2A 5X3

**Are you a current subscriber to Love Inspired® Suspense books
and want to receive the larger-print edition?
Call 1-800-873-8635 or visit www.ReaderService.com.**

* Terms and prices subject to change without notice. Prices do not include applicable taxes. Sales tax applicable in N.Y. Canadian residents will be charged applicable taxes. Offer not valid in Quebec. This offer is limited to one order per household. Not valid for current subscribers to Love Inspired Suspense larger-print books. All orders subject to credit approval. Credit or debit balances in a customer's account(s) may be offset by any other outstanding balance owed by or to the customer. Please allow 4 to 6 weeks for delivery. Offer available while quantities last.

Your Privacy—The Reader Service is committed to protecting your privacy. Our Privacy Policy is available online at www.ReaderService.com or upon request from the Reader Service.

We make a portion of our mailing list available to reputable third parties that offer products we believe may interest you. If you prefer that we not exchange your name with third parties, or if you wish to clarify or modify your communication preferences, please visit us at www.ReaderService.com/consumerschoice or write to us at Reader Service Preference Service, P.O. Box 9062, Buffalo, NY 14240-9062. Include your complete name and address.

LISLP15

REQUEST YOUR FREE BOOKS!
2 FREE WHOLESOME ROMANCE NOVELS IN LARGER PRINT
PLUS 2 FREE MYSTERY GIFTS

HEARTWARMING™

Wholesome, tender romances

YES! Please send me 2 FREE Harlequin® Heartwarming Larger-Print novels and my 2 FREE mystery gifts (gifts worth about $10). After receiving them, if I don't wish to receive any more books, I can return the shipping statement marked "cancel." If I don't cancel, I will receive 4 brand-new larger-print novels every month and be billed just $5.24 per book in the U.S. or $5.99 per book in Canada. That's a savings of at least 19% off the cover price. It's quite a bargain! Shipping and handling is just 50¢ per book in the U.S. and 75¢ per book in Canada.* I understand that accepting the 2 free books and gifts places me under no obligation to buy anything. I can always return a shipment and cancel at any time. Even if I never buy another book, the two free books and gifts are mine to keep forever.

161/361 IDN GHX2

Name	(PLEASE PRINT)	
Address		Apt. #
City	State/Prov.	Zip/Postal Code

Signature (if under 18, a parent or guardian must sign)

Mail to the **Reader Service**:
IN U.S.A.: P.O. Box 1867, Buffalo, NY 14240-1867
IN CANADA: P.O. Box 609, Fort Erie, Ontario L2A 5X3

* Terms and prices subject to change without notice. Prices do not include applicable taxes. Sales tax applicable in N.Y. Canadian residents will be charged applicable taxes. Offer not valid in Quebec. This offer is limited to one order per household. Not valid for current subscribers to Harlequin Heartwarming larger-print books. All orders subject to credit approval. Credit or debit balances in a customer's account(s) may be offset by any other outstanding balance owed by or to the customer. Please allow 4 to 6 weeks for delivery. Offer available while quantities last.

Your Privacy—The Reader Service is committed to protecting your privacy. Our Privacy Policy is available online at www.ReaderService.com or upon request from the Reader Service.

We make a portion of our mailing list available to reputable third parties that offer products we believe may interest you. If you prefer that we not exchange your name with third parties, or if you wish to clarify or modify your communication preferences, please visit us at www.ReaderService.com/consumerschoice or write to us at Reader Service Preference Service, P.O. Box 9062, Buffalo, NY 14240-9062. Include your complete name and address.

HW15

WESTERN WP PROMISES

YES! Please send me **The Western Promises Collection** in Larger Print. This collection begins with 3 FREE books and 2 FREE gifts (gifts valued at approx. $14.00 retail) in the first shipment, along with the other first 4 books from the collection! If I do not cancel, I will receive 8 monthly shipments until I have the entire 51-book Western Promises collection. I will receive 2 or 3 FREE books in each shipment and I will pay just $4.99 US/ $5.89 CDN for each of the other four books in each shipment, plus $2.99 for shipping and handling per shipment. *If I decide to keep the entire collection, I'll have paid for only 32 books, because 19 books are FREE! I understand that accepting the 3 free books and gifts places me under no obligation to buy anything. I can always return a shipment and cancel at any time. My free books and gifts are mine to keep no matter what I decide.

272 HCN 3070 472 HCN 3070

Name	(PLEASE PRINT)
Address	Apt. #
City	State/Prov.	Zip/Postal Code

Signature (if under 18, a parent or guardian must sign)

Mail to the **Reader Service**:
IN U.S.A.: P.O. Box 1867, Buffalo, NY 14240-1867
IN CANADA: P.O. Box 609, Fort Erie, Ontario L2A 5X3

* Terms and prices subject to change without notice. Prices do not include applicable taxes. Sales tax applicable in N.Y. Canadian residents will be charged applicable taxes. This offer is limited to one order per household. All orders subject to approval. Credit or debit balances in a customer's account(s) may be offset by any other outstanding balance owed by or to the customer. Please allow 4 to 6 weeks for delivery. Offer available while quantities last. Offer not available to Quebec residents.

READERSERVICE.COM

Manage your account online!

- Review your order history
- Manage your payments
- Update your address

*We've designed the
Reader Service website
just for you.*

Enjoy all the features!

- Discover new series available to you, and read excerpts from any series.
- Respond to mailings and special monthly offers.
- Connect with favorite authors at the blog.
- Browse the Bonus Bucks catalog and online-only exculsives.
- Share your feedback.

Visit us at:
ReaderService.com